ALSO BY RUTH WHITE

The Treasure of Way Down Deep

Little Audrey

Way Down Deep

The Search for Belle Prater

Buttermilk Hill

Tadpole

Memories of Summer

Belle Prater's Boy

Weeping Willow

Sweet Creek Holler

A MONTH *of* SUNDAYS

A
MONTH
of
SUNDAYS

Ruth White

SQUARE
FISH

FARRAR STRAUS GIROUX
NEW YORK

SQUARE FISH

An Imprint of Macmillan
175 Fifth Avenue
New York, NY 10010
mackids.com

Square Fish and the Square Fish logo are trademarks of Macmillan and
are used by Farrar Straus Giroux under license from Macmillan.

Square Fish books may be purchased for business or promotional use. For infor-
mation on bulk purchases, please contact the Macmillan Corporate and Premium Sales
Department at (800) 221-7945 x 5442 or by e-mail at specialmarkets@macmillan.com.

Lyrics on page 106 from "It Is No Secret" by Stuart Hamblen © 1950, renewed
© 1977 by Hamblen Music Company. All rights reserved. International copyright
secured. Member of CCLI and ASCAP—www.HamblenMusic.com

Library of Congress Cataloging-in-Publication Data
White, Ruth.
A month of Sundays / Ruth White.
    p. cm.
ISBN 978-1-250-02730-6
[1. Families—Fiction.   2. Sick—Fiction.   3. Family problems—Fiction.
4. Christianity—Fiction.   5. Country life—Virginia—Fiction.   6. Virginia—
History—20th century—Fiction.]   I. Title.

PZ7.W58446Mo 2011   [Fic]—dc22   2010036311

Originally published in the United States by Farrar Straus Giroux
First Square Fish Edition: July 2013
Square Fish logo designed by Filomena Tuosto

10   9   8   7   6   5   4   3   2   1

AR: 4.0 / LEXILE: 680L

For Margaret

A MONTH *of* SUNDAYS

I

Before I was born fourteen years ago, my dad, August Rose, left my mom, Betty Rose, for a carnival singer. With no close kin, and nobody to help her in a pinch, Mom had to take some pretty lousy jobs over the years. Of course, living in Elkhorn City, Kentucky, where nobody lives a posh life, her expectations were not that high to start with.

For the last few years Mom has been working in a grocery store. Above the market is a three-room dump where we live with a woman named Lily, who also works in the store. Yes, it gets pretty crowded, and I do resent it.

I have asked Mom maybe a hundred times why she doesn't chase my dad down and wring some money out of him, but she has been too stubborn and proud to do that. So while I've been wearing last year's shoes and dreaming over dresses in the Sears catalog that I'll never have, Mom has clung to her precious pride, like it's worth more than me.

Recently, Mom's childhood friend, Grace Colley, came back to Elkhorn City after a long absence, but immediately began to wish she hadn't. So do I. She and Mom are thick as thieves.

It's the last week of school, and I come home one day to find them at the kitchen table with their heads together, doing some figuring on a piece of paper. And I can tell by their expressions that something is going on.

When Mom looks up and sees me, she says with excitement in her voice, "Garnet, I have finally got enough money saved to get out of here. We're going to Florida!"

"Florida? You mean to live?"

"If I can find work there, yes. They've been talking on the radio about Daytona Beach. It's the hot place for jobs right now."

I sit down at the table. Florida!

"When are we leaving?"

Mom does not answer right away, and her eyes meet Grace's.

"Garnet, honey," Mom says at last. "I was thinking that maybe Grace and I would go first, and find work. When I've saved enough, I'll send bus fare money, and you can join us down there. It shouldn't take long once I have a job."

All my blood rushes to my face. "So that's what you were thinking, huh? You're going to leave me here with Lily?"

"No, of course not. I've written a letter to your dad's sister, June, asking her if you can stay with her."

"But we don't even know each other!"

"It's time to remedy that situation," Mom says.

"Why can't I go with you?"

"Chiefly because of the expense," Mom says. "Three people on the road costs more than two. We're going on a shoestring as it is."

I can only glare at her because there are certain things you can't say to your mom, no matter how mad you are.

"Besides," Mom goes on, "you would have to stay by yourself a lot while we're looking for work, and I would worry about you in a strange place."

And it's settled. Do I have any say in the matter? Do I ever?

Aunt June answers Mom's letter right away, saying she had absolutely no idea her brother had a child.

"Why on earth would August keep something like that from me?" she says in her letter. "Of course Otis and I would be thrilled to meet April Garnet, and look after her while you are finding work in Florida."

She says she's sorry August will not be there to see me, but she has no idea where that rascal is. He has not been around in more than a year.

The following Sunday we are in Grace's Packard on our way to Black River, Virginia, about two hours from Elkhorn City, where I will live among strangers for an indefinite period of time. I don't speak to Mom all the way there.

"I'm sure this is her house," Mom says when we arrive and find nobody home. "I remember how it hangs out into the road, because it's built on a curve. And how could I ever forget this funny green color?"

I finally have to break my silence. "Didn't you tell her we were coming today?"

"Not exactly," Mom says. "I just told her sometime this weekend."

I do an exaggerated eye roll, then turn my back to her.

"Don't be so grumpy!" Mom says.

We take my suitcase from Grace's car, and the three of us sit down in some chairs on the porch. Grace looks at her watch. It's clear she wants to hightail it out of here as soon as she can. It's a pretty busy road here, and some of the cars slow down to look at us as they pass. Not only that, but there are houses lining both sides of the road, and people are craning their necks to see out the windows. Some of them even come outside.

I guess they can't stand not knowing who we are. Directly across the road is a small brick store that says Richards' Grocery on the window. A man and woman are sitting in rocking chairs out front.

The sun is hiding behind a rising storm cloud. A wind begins to stir the trees on the hills that rise up all around this valley.

"Hey, y'all! Yoo-hoo!"

It's a woman waving at us from the house beside the store.

"Wonder what she wants?" Mom says, and raises her hand to wave back.

"Are you waiting on Otis and June Bill?" the woman calls.

"Yes we are!" Mom replies.

"Well, they went to the cemetery to lay flowers on the graves of their kin."

Right. It's Decoration Day.

"But they should be back here drek'ly," the woman goes on. "Who are y'all anyhow?"

Mom sighs. "I'll go talk to her."

And she leaves the porch to cross the road and speak with the nosy woman. In a few moments Mom comes back.

"That's Mrs. Mays," she says. "And those two in the rocking chairs are Mr. and Mrs. Richards, who own the store. They are just tickled to death to meet

August's *wife*." Mom smirks as she emphasizes the word "wife."

Technically, Mom is still Dad's wife since they never got a divorce.

"They will be even more tickled to meet August's little girl whenever she feels like coming over to see them."

"August's little girl?" I say sourly. "I wonder how many times I'll have to hear that?"

Mom and Grace laugh at me. They are in a jolly mood. Well, good for them!

"And I learned June and Otis have two boys," Mom says. "Their names are Emory and Avery."

The rain starts coming down in big sparkling drops, and still we wait for more than an hour. Finally a brand-new '57 Plymouth Fury, nearly the same color as the house, comes rolling up beside the porch. Inside there's a man driving, and a woman on the seat beside him. In the back are two good-sized boys, maybe ten and twelve. Must be the Bills, my long-lost kin.

2

Aunt June is a little bitty woman, no more than five feet tall and about a hundred pounds. Uncle Otis is big and burly with a bushy beard on his face. He looks like a gorilla. The boys are ordinary-looking. Everybody has blue eyes.

"I'll declare! I'll declare!" Aunt June says as she pulls Mom into a hug. "Good to see you again, Betty."

Uncle Otis silently shakes Mom's hand, the boys mumble something, Mom introduces Grace, then they all turn to me.

"And this is your niece, April Garnet Rose," Mom says to Aunt June.

I try to smile at my dad's sister. After all, none of this is her fault.

"August's little girl!" she says, and hugs me. There it

is again. Then she stands back and studies me. "I think you have your daddy's eyes, but you look more like your mom."

Mom and Grace keep edging toward the porch steps. They can't wait to get away.

"Y'all come in and have something to eat and drink," Aunt June says to them. "You don't want to leave in this rain."

"We really need to hit the road," Mom says. "We've got a long drive ahead of us."

Grace nods in agreement and glances at her watch again.

"Well, don't worry about April Garnet. We'll take good care of her."

Mom looks at me, then comes over and puts an arm around me.

"I promise to write, sweetie, as soon as I have an address where you can reach me," she says. "Then we can make arrangements for you to join us." And she kisses me on the cheek. "Now, don't you cry, hear me?"

"I'm not crying," I mumble.

"You look like you're about to."

"Well, I'm not! Go on, get out of here!"

And just like that, Mom and Grace are gone.

"I'll declare, I'll declare," Aunt June mumbles.

I'm guessing it's something she says when she can't think of anything else to say.

"Why did your mama bring you here?" the older boy says rudely.

"Hush, now, Emory," Aunt June says to him. "She's your first cousin."

"I thought Madge was our first cousin," says the small boy—Avery, I guess.

"Madge is your first cousin and so is April," Aunt June says.

"That don't make sense," says Avery. "Somebody has to be second."

"I've always been called Garnet," I inform Aunt June, though I've never known why Mom insists on using my middle name.

"Oh, okay, Garnet. We're glad to have you here, aren't we, Otis?"

She turns to her husband, who hasn't yet spoken a word.

"Oh, yeah, sure," he manages to say. "It's a nice surprise."

Surprise? So he didn't know I was coming? It sounds like the boys didn't know either.

"Let's get in out of the rain," Aunt June says. "Emory, take her suitcase."

"Take her suitcase?" he sputters. "Where to?"

"Go on now," Aunt June coaxes him. "Take her suitcase in the house for her. It won't hurt you to do that."

"I'll carry it myself," I say as I grab the suitcase by the handle. "I don't need help."

We go in the house. It's a very strange place. There are rooms shooting off in all directions. It's a maze— that's what it is. Right in the middle of the maze are wooden stairs. I can't tell what's at the top.

"Avery, show Garnet up to the sunporch," Aunt June says.

I wonder what a sunporch is, but I'll not ask.

"Come on, Garnet," Avery says, and I am glad to see he's a friendly, smiling little thing, not a bit like Emory.

Upstairs there are short hallways running in four directions. We turn down one of them to the left and wind up in a room that looks like it was just glued onto the end of the house. The first thing that hits you is all the yellow—a yellow bedspread on a double bed, a yellow skirt on a vanity table, and one yellow wall. The other three sides of the room are big windows with yellow and white café curtains. Rain is slashing against the glass.

"This is our sunporch," Avery says proudly. "Daddy just made it for Mama the other day."

"The other day?"

"I mean he finished it the other day. He's been building on it for a long time."

"It's nice," I say. I mean it. I love it. I don't think I ever saw a brighter room in my life. And I'll bet when the sun shines in here you could get a tan just lying on the bed.

I put my suitcase down and turn to see myself in a mirror over the vanity table beside the door. My face is pale, my shoulder-length blond hair is messy, and my blue eyes have faint shadows under them.

"You sure are pretty," Avery says to me suddenly, and I am so surprised I am speechless. Now, I really feel like I'm going to cry, but I don't.

3

I follow Avery back the way we came.

"How many rooms in this house?" I ask him.

"I don't know."

I count six closed doors on this floor.

"That's the bathroom," he says, and points to a door at the end of one of the hallways. "Just in case you ever need to go."

I follow him down the stairs, then through the front hall into a dining room. I hear a telephone ringing somewhere, and a muffled voice answers. We enter the biggest kitchen in the world, where Aunt June has put on an apron and is starting to cook. Emory is at a monster-sized wooden table reading the funny papers, and Uncle Otis is nowhere. It must have been him answering the phone.

This kitchen is so roomy, there's a large stone fireplace along the right wall and a massive red leather couch, a coffee table, and two arm chairs in front of it. I get a brief vision of a winter evening with a roaring fire going. Bet it's cozy in here then.

Avery sits down at the big table, so I sit there too.

Aunt June smiles at me. "After a while, if it stops raining, we'll go out in the backyard, you and me, and have us a talk, okay?"

"Okay."

"It'll be nice to have a girl to talk to instead of all these men," she says, and smiles again. "Do you like the sunporch?"

"Yeah, it's pretty."

I hear the phone ringing again.

"Have you ever had shrimp?" Aunt June says.

"No."

"Well, that's what we're having for supper."

"What does it taste like?"

"I don't know. I never had it either. We got this new freezer a few weeks ago, and it came stocked full of food. Some of it we never heard of. But we like to try different things."

"Bet you don't even know what a freezer is," Emory says. It seems he's just itching for a fight, but he won't get one from me.

"My mom worked in a grocery store," I say calmly. "They had freezers."

"Well, come out here and see our freezer," Aunt June says. "I'm proud of it."

I follow Aunt June to a screened porch, which I am calculating is smack underneath the sunporch. Here you can see and hear the traffic splashing through the rain. The freezer is standing tall and white against the wall, and when Aunt June opens it I see it is full of packages of foods froze to rocks.

"That's how it was delivered to us," Aunt June says, "stocked full. They do that to make them sell better. Some of it's ordinary stuff like green beans and corn, but some of it's uncommon, like the shrimp. We have oysters too, and asparagus. You ever had asparagus?"

I shake my head.

Aunt June lifts out several packages and shows them to me. They have writing on them, and some of them have pictures to match the words. Broccoli, cauliflower, creamed spinach, crab cakes, filet mignon. Filet mignon?

I follow her back into the kitchen.

"Do you like Pogo?" Emory asks me, looking up from the comics.

"Not much," I say back.

"Who do you like?" he wants to know.

"Li'l Abner."

"I can't stand Li'l Abner. He's stupid."

Aunt June cooks the shrimp with butter and boils

some potatoes. She adds to that a mess of sugar peas and some crispy new radishes, both fresh out of her garden, she says. Everything looks good and I realize I have not had a bite since about ten o'clock this morning, and now it's around five in the evening.

"Hungry?" Aunt June asks, like she's reading my mind.

"I could eat the legs off this table."

That was not a bit original, just something I've heard other people say, so I'm surprised when Aunt June and Avery bust out laughing.

Then Aunt June says to Avery, "Go tell your daddy supper's ready."

Avery does what she says, and in a minute he comes back in with his daddy behind him. Uncle Otis scratches his beard, sits down at the table, and folds his hands before him.

"Earth that gave us all this food," Aunt June begins, and all heads go down. "Sun that made it ripe and good. Dearest Earth, dearest sun, we'll not forget what you have done."

She passes the shrimp around, then asks Uncle Otis, "Who was on the phone?"

"Neighbors," Uncle Otis responds. "Wanting to know about the girl."

Except for the clattering of our forks against the plates, silence follows. The shrimp is a new taste, but I like it. It seems everybody likes it, except for Emory, and he pretends to be gagging on it.

Aunt June tries to make conversation. "We are celebrating our centennial this year," she tells me. "That's why your uncle Otis has grown a beard. A lot of men in the county are growing them, and on the Fourth of July there will be a big celebration. That's when they will give a prize for the best beard."

"Bet you don't know what a centennial is!" Emory says to me, and he laughs with his mouth open. I can see peas and potatoes in there. It's disgusting.

The phone is ringing again, and everybody ignores it.

"A centennial is a birthday of one hundred years," Aunt June explains. "That's how old our county is this year."

It's about all the conversation we get. I eat like I never had food before, and they watch me like they never saw a girl eat before. Then Uncle Otis finishes his supper and leaves the kitchen. He still has not spoken directly to me, and I can't help but wonder what he's thinking.

4

I help Aunt June do dishes and clean up the kitchen. I don't know where anything goes, but I guess I'll learn. The rain has stopped, and we go out to the backyard like Aunt June said we would. Avery wants to come, but she tells him sweetly that she wants a private talk with her niece.

Avery is disappointed, but he says, "Oh, all right."

It's nice out. Everything smells fresh after the rain. There's a picnic table and there's a hammock hung between two apple trees. Aunt June shows her garden to me, and it looks like it might be the devil to work in. That's because part of it runs up the side of a hill.

From here I can see the house better, and it looks like a jigsaw puzzle that was put together wrong. You can tell where the sunporch and several other rooms were added on to the main house.

Aunt June has brought a rag to dry off the picnic table. We sit there and she asks me a bunch of questions. Where do I go to school? What grade am I in? Do I make good grades? What is Elkhorn City like? Then she asks me what Mom has been up to all these years. She says they met only once before when my dad brought her here for a visit.

"She's still just as pretty as she was then," Aunt June says. "I remember how August lost his head over her."

Yeah, my mom is pretty. Everybody says so. But I've never known anybody to lose his head over her. And if he was so crazy about her, why did he leave? But I don't say any of that. What's the point?

"Do you think she's still mad at August for leaving?" she wants to know.

I hesitate to answer, because the truth is I don't know how Mom feels about my dad. She has rarely said a nice thing about him. But I remember a night some years ago when I woke up and saw her standing at the window with the moonlight pouring in around her. She was crying, and I heard her say one word. I think it was "August." Mom was not aware that I saw her like that. She'd be mortified.

I shrug and say, "I don't know."

Now Aunt June wants to know if I have any questions for her.

"Yeah, how come your house is so close to that busy road?"

Aunt June smiles. "When this house was built more than a hundred years ago, it was a one-room log cabin put up right smack in the middle of the woods. You can still see the logs in there. And not another house was in sight of it. There was no road either, just a path going to the doorway. Over the years other people built, and the road got wider. As you can see, this valley is so narrow there's barely enough room for a big road like that and a row of houses on each side of it too."

"So did y'all add all the rooms to the log cabin?"

"We bought this house from January Rose, my dad. He added the four rooms downstairs when he and Mama were raising me and August. Otis and I added the second floor, where there are five bedrooms, counting the sunporch, and a bath. Someday we will probably turn the dining room into something else. We don't ever use it to eat in."

"That's interesting," I say, and we sit there studying the house. "Are your mama and dad still living?"

"Mama died when Avery was a baby," Aunt June says. "But Dad is living in Bluefield. Emory and Avery call him Poppy. He's your poppy too, and I'm sure y'all will get to meet each other pretty soon. He visits a lot these days."

So I do have a grandpa, and I'll get to meet him. Mom didn't know if my grandparents were still alive.

"As for your dad," Aunt June says with a sigh, then

smiles, apparently at the thought of him. "Well, have you heard that song 'The Happy Wanderer'?"

"Yeah, we sang it in school."

"That's been the life of August Rose ever since he left your mom—the happy wanderer. He drifts here, drifts there. And he won't keep in touch."

"Is he still with that carnival singer?" I ask Aunt June.

"What carnival singer?"

"You know, the one he . . ."

Aunt June's face is a blank. Maybe she really doesn't know that story. I hope she'll let me drop the subject. She does.

I think about the names. January Rose. June Rose. August Rose. And me—April Garnet Rose. We got a third of the calendar covered. Why would my mom follow the Rose family tradition even after my dad left her?

"Why don't Emory and Avery have calendar names?" I ask.

"Otis wouldn't hear of it," Aunt June says. "They have old Bill family names. Now, Garnet, I want you to know that I'm glad to have you here, and I hope you'll enjoy your visit."

I feel like smiling now, so I do, and I say, "Thank you." Then I add, "Don't worry. Mom will send for me like she said, as soon as she can."

"I'm not a bit worried," Aunt June says, and pats my hand. "Let's go in and watch television."

Television! Wow! I didn't know they had a television. Lily had a radio, and we listened to shows every night. I've also seen quite a few movies, because it only costs a quarter, but I have never watched television before.

I follow Aunt June into the house, through the screened porch and kitchen, through the dining room and front hallway, past the stairs, and into a living room. It's such a pretty room, all decorated in gold, brown, dark red, and deep forest green.

"Why, it looks like October!" I say to Aunt June, and she seems pleased.

The telephone is here on a table, but I don't see a television. We keep going and come to a smaller living room. That's where we find that flickering screen and the rest of the family. There are two plush couches and two big easy chairs all jumbled up together in this room. I suspected before, but now I am fairly certain, that my aunt and uncle are well off, at least better off than most folks I know.

I sit on one of the easy chairs, and it's so soft, I feel like I'm going to sink through it to the floor. First we watch the news, then *Lassie*, followed by Jack Benny. He makes me laugh out loud.

After a while Aunt June says to Avery, "You can run to the store now."

And Avery gets up to go.

"You be careful crossing that road," Aunt June hollers after him.

Pretty soon Avery comes back with Pepsi-Colas and 5th Avenue candy bars for everybody. He gives me mine first, and I thank him.

The Ed Sullivan Show comes on, and I don't think I ever saw anything so entertaining. I believe I could watch television all night. During a commercial I feel eyes on me. I try to keep from noticing, but it's like bugs crawling over my skin. So I glance around the room, and there they are, all of them staring at me like I'm more interesting than the television! Then they look away quick.

Next *General Electric Theater* comes on, followed by *Alfred Hitchcock Presents* and *The $64,000 Challenge.* I'm surprised Aunt June does not tell us to go to bed. But we stay on through *What's My Line?* Nobody makes a move to turn in until "The Star-Spangled Banner" plays at eleven o'clock, the television station signs off, and the test pattern comes on.

Then we go up the stairs, and Aunt June and Avery tell me good night and sleep tight. I go into the yellow room, close the door, and lean against it with my eyes closed. I start to turn on the light, then I think of all the windows in here. The café curtains are not enough to hide behind. There are still a few cars passing by, and people could see me taking off my clothes if they looked. I feel like I've been onstage all evening, and I don't plan to give anybody else a show tonight. So I undress down to my petticoat in the dark, pull back the bedspread, and slip between soft yellow sheets.

I lie in the bed looking at the sky and wonder about Mom. How far did they get today? Maybe North Carolina. Where are they sleeping tonight? Maybe in the car.

I need to go to the bathroom. I hope I don't stump my toe in the dark. One time I did that, and my toe never was right again. It went all crooked. I go down the hall as quiet and careful as I can. I hear voices behind one of the doors, and I stop to listen. It's Uncle Otis.

"You should have told me, June."

"Maybe, but I knew you'd say no, and I just had to see her," Aunt June responds. "She's August's little girl"

"You're right. I would've said no. She's way too much for you to take on right now," Uncle Otis says.

Aunt June says something back, but I hurry away without making a sound and find the bathroom.

When I'm in bed again, I say to myself, "Well, April Garnet Rose, your mom's gone, and you might as well get used to it, because you got nobody in the world now, except the inhabitants of this derned old puke green house, and at least half of them think you're way too much trouble."

5

When I come awake, it feels like it's late in the morning, but I don't hear a sound in the house. I get up and open my suitcase. That's when I find that Mom has slipped in a package of pink stationery for me, along with some postage stamps, and a small snapshot of herself clipped to a note that says, "I love you."

"Like I know where to send a letter!" I say crossly, and shove those items into my nightstand drawer.

Then I find fresh underwear and a pair of shorts and a shirt. In the bathroom there are clean washcloths and towels, so I run some water in the tub and take a bath. It's soothing.

When I'm dressed I step lightly into the hall. I still don't hear or see anybody. Back on the sunporch, I make up my bed before tiptoeing down the steps. At the bottom I go left and into the October room so I can see it again. I glance out the front window at Richards' Grocery, then walk around, admiring and touching stuff.

There's a small fireplace here with a mantel lined with family pictures. Here's one of Avery, one of Emory, and one . . . ? And there he is in black-and-white, the man I know nothing about except that he left my mom for a carnival singer. If Mom had a picture of him, she never showed it to me, but I know it's him. He looks like Aunt June, and maybe I do have his eyes. He is smiling into the camera, and he is so good-looking I could cry.

I am suddenly filled with an anger I can't explain.

"Why did you leave us?" I whisper to him through clenched teeth. "Things might have been different if you, if only you . . ."

I don't know how to finish, because I really don't understand what happened between my mom and dad those years ago when they were expecting me. I swallow my feelings and turn away quickly. I feel his eyes following me as I leave the room.

Standing in the hall again, I see a door behind the stairs that I didn't notice last night because it was in the shadows. It looks like it's real old, made of heavy, dark boards with big pegs holding it together instead of nails. It must be the original log cabin Aunt June told me about. I try the handle, but the door is locked.

I wander into the kitchen, but I don't think I should

be poking around in Aunt June's cabinets to see what I can find to eat. I'll wait till everybody is up. In the meantime, I'll sit in the sun, which is shining bright. There is not one cloud in the sky, and the birds are singing like they're on the radio. If I were back home, I would feel good on a day like this. I would go about my business humming a tune.

But this is not my home, and it seems I'm not altogether welcome here. I'm glad the Plymouth is not parked beside the house. That means Uncle Otis is gone, probably to work.

After a while I see a fat girl peeping over a wire fence that separates her yard from Aunt June's. Her hair is orange as a pumpkin, and her freckles have got freckles. I figure she's about fifteen or sixteen.

"Hidy, girl," she calls to me. "I heered somebody say you're June's niece. Where you live at?"

"Elkhorn City."

"Where's that at?"

"Kentucky."

"Yeah, I been there three times—or two—I reckon."

I wonder if she's quite right in the head.

"My Irish kin lives there," she goes on.

I say nothing.

"I'm half Irish."

With all that red hair, I can believe it.

"I'm half German too," she tells me. "My last name is Fritz. And I'm half American."

"That's three halfs," I say.

"Yeah," she says. "I'm big."

That gets a smile out of me. "What's your first name?"

"Mitzi."

I tell her my name, and she says, "Garnet, maybe you and me can buddy up. Ain't nothing but boys around here. You hankering to buddy up with me?"

I don't know what to say to that.

"But Mommy won't let me git outside this fence," Mitzi says. " 'Cause I'm apt to go a'wanderin'."

"Garnet!" Aunt June is calling to me from the kitchen window. "I'm fixing to cook us some breakfast."

"Yeah, I'll be your buddy, Mitzi," I tell her. I figure boys are not nice to her, and she needs a friend as much as I do.

"See you later, alligator!" she hollers as I go toward the house.

"After while, crocodile!" I call back.

"So you've met Mitzi?" Aunt June says as I go into the kitchen.

I nod.

"She's a card," Aunt June comments with a smile. "A real card."

"Is she all there?" I ask.

"Not quite," Aunt June answers. "They say something happened when she was born. I don't know what. But she's a real sweet girl."

Aunt June lays bacon strips in a skillet.

"You know, Garnet, I've been thinking it over ever since your mom asked me to keep you, and now that you're here, I know why."

"Why what?"

"Why this has all come about. You see, I think there's a reason for everything, whether we know it or not, and you came here to help me find God. I've been searching for him for months now."

"Why?"

"Why not? Don't you want to know if he's real?"

I shrug. "I've never puzzled over it much. How do you search?"

"I try a different church every week. Yesterday I was at Big Branch, and last week I went to Little Prater. Now I'll have you to go with me and help."

Mom and I were never churchgoing types. I've gone only a few times with school friends. As for what I believe, I couldn't say, but I kinda doubt that God would disrupt my life like this just so Aunt June would have somebody to go to church with.

But what I say out loud is, "How am I supposed to help?"

"You can give me moral support, and also I'll get new insight from fresh eyes. I can't get Otis to go, and the boys? Well, Avery is too young, and you see how Emory is."

Imagine that. She's his mother and she sees how he is.

"How old is Emory anyhow?"

"He's twelve and Avery's nine."

So my guess was close.

"Next Sunday," Aunt June goes on, "I'm going to the Joy Creek Church of Jesus. They're going to speak in tongues."

"Do what?"

"That's right! They talk in unknown languages."

"What for?"

"They get the Holy Ghost. It's part of their worship. Don't you want to see that?"

I roll my eyes.

"It'll be inspirational, you'll see."

"Sure," I say. "And about as useful as a back pocket on a shirt."

Aunt June chuckles. Yeah, I'll have to say she's pretty good-natured.

6

It's just me and Avery and Aunt June for breakfast.

"Hey, Garnet," Avery says. "Did you hear the one about the invisible man and the invisible woman getting married?"

I shake my head.

"Well, their young'uns were nothing to look at either."

Actually, I've heard that corny joke before, but I laugh to make him feel good. He laughs harder than I do.

"Where is Emory and Uncle Otis?" I ask.

"Emory's still sleeping," Aunt June says. "He'd sleep all day, if I let him. And your uncle went off to work early on."

"What kind of work does Uncle Otis do?"

"Uncle Dewey has a shop up at his house, where him and Daddy make starting boxes," Avery says, and I can tell he's proud. "They're making about a million thousand dollars selling 'em."

"Don't exaggerate," Aunt June tells him. Then she explains. "Your uncle and his brother, Dewey, have invented a starting box for the rail cars that go back into the coal mines. I understand that it acts something like an electrical transformer. The machinery is direct current, or DC. The starting box controls the amount of voltage going into the motor to prevent a sudden surge of electricity coming in at the start-up. They are compact, not much bigger than a shoe box, and the core elements are hardwood posts lined with copper straps. They are a great improvement over the old ones, and everybody wants one."

"Wow!" is all I can think to say, because I'm impressed and astonished by Aunt June's knowledge of Uncle Otis's work.

She grins at me and says, "It runs on both sides of the family—this interest in anything electrical. Your poppy and your dad are electricians, and so are Otis and his brother. If I were a man, I'd probably be one too."

"My dad is an electrician?" I ask.

"He sure is. He went back to school and got certified."

"Uncle Dewey has a girl four years old," Avery says. "Her name is Madge."

"And that's your other first cousin?" I ask him.

"No, she's my second cousin now. You're my first."

Aunt June and I smile at each other. If it were only these two I had to put up with, I wouldn't mind being here at all.

By the time we finish breakfast it's almost eleven. Emory drags his carcass out of bed in time to eat the leftovers, and he's still grumpy. I want to get away from him, so I wander toward the front rooms. Avery follows me.

"Can I look in there?" I ask him about the door behind the stairs.

"No. God's in there."

I stop short, put my hands on my hips, and give him the eye. "Well, you better tell your mama. She's been looking all over for him!"

Avery laughs. "I mean it's locked 'cause it's where Mama keeps her God stuff, and she goes there to pray."

"God stuff?"

"You know, her Bible and books. And she hides things in there—secret things."

That's interesting. A room for secrets.

In the afternoon Aunt June makes me and Avery and Emory help weed the garden. Emory manages to manipulate me so that I get the patch running up the hill.

Like I figured, it's awkward. You have to brace yourself against falling while trying to hoe at the same time.

Aunt June is wearing a broad-brimmed straw hat. She is pouring sweat in the sun, and she takes off the hat to fan herself with it. Her face is brick red, and I think if people around here would get out of bed before noon, we wouldn't have to work in the hot sun. We could do it early in the morning. But I manage—with considerable effort—to hold my tongue. Then Aunt June quits before finishing her row and goes to the hammock, which is shaded by the apple trees. She looks like a little girl lying there.

I am surprised when Emory goes to where she is and bends over her. They speak for a few moments; then Emory goes into the house and brings out water for her. I gotta admit that was a pretty sweet thing for him to do.

Aunt June recovers after resting and has supper ready when Uncle Otis comes home from work around five-thirty. As it turns out, filet mignon is nothing more than cow meat, but it's so tender, even if you were toothless you could gum it to pieces.

The evening goes about the same as yesterday. We eat. Then we go to the television room. When it's time for pop and candy, Avery asks me if I want to go to the store with him. I say I guess so.

"Y'all be careful crossing that road," Aunt June hollers after us. And we are.

The store is cramped and dark. It smells like old wood and something pungent—turpentine, maybe. There's not much on the shelves.

Mr. Richards laughs when he sees me. "Well, there she is! August's little girl!"

"Her name's Garnet," Avery says.

"Pleased to meet you, Garnet," Mr. Richards says. Up close I can see that he's a tall, thin, white-headed old geezer with flabby jaws hanging like a bloodhound's.

"It's a pretty name," Mrs. Richards says. She is short and humpbacked, a funny-looking wee woman. Her hair is dyed a reddish brown, but there's about an inch of gray at the roots.

"We knew August when he was a boy," Mr. Richards says. "He was a ball of energy."

"I'll pick the pop, Garnet," Avery says as he peeps into the drink cooler, "and you can pick the candy."

I look over the selection of candy. Not much to choose from. I decide on Hershey bars as Avery pulls five bottles of Royal Crown Cola out of the cooler. Mrs. Richards places everything in two brown paper pokes.

"Charge it," Avery says as we head out the door.

"How long you stayin' for?" Mrs. Richards calls, but Avery and I are darting across the road before the words are out of her mouth.

7

It's Thursday morning, and I'm sitting on the ground facing Mitzi with the wire fence between us. We've been meeting each morning, and I like her more every time I see her. Oh, I know it—she's not all together. She looks like Raggedy Ann, and she has a hillbilly drawl thick enough to spread on a biscuit, but she's my friend. She's easy to talk to. I just hate that she can't go to school with the other kids. That's what she told me. People say she's too dumb to get educated. That hurts her feelings.

"Emory's not friendly with me," I am telling her. "But Avery is sweet."

Mitzi is chewing on a ham biscuit. It looks so good. I'm hungry, and Aunt June is still in bed. I think I might have to start finding my own breakfast.

"Yeah, Avery's tenderhearted," Mitzi agrees. "Emory's got thangs weighing on him."

"Like what?"

"Beats me, but I kin tell. Emory's burdened in his mind."

"About what?" I persist.

"Dunno. He useta laugh till he pooted," Mitzi says.

At that I laugh.

"It's the truth," Mitzi says. "Him and his daddy too."

"Uncle Otis?" I say. "I can't imagine him laughing much."

"He kin act the fool good as anybody," Mitzi tells me.

I think about it all day. They used to laugh, and now they don't. Wonder how long ago that was? Could it be only last week, and now they don't laugh on account of me?

When Uncle Otis comes home from work he brings in a handful of mail and begins to sort it on the kitchen table.

"Postcard for you, Garnet," he says to me, "from your mom."

Well, what about that. He has finally spoken directly to me. And he sounds almost friendly. The postcard shows a picture of Daytona Beach, addressed to Garnet Rose, in care of Otis Bill, State Road 460, Black River, VA.

Hello, Garnet.

We got here all right, and Grace has got herself a job already. I'm still looking. You will like it here. Write to me at the address below and tell me what's going on. I hope you are having a good time. Tell your aunt and uncle hello for me. See you soon.

Love, Mom

I'll like it there? Sure, whenever she decides she wants to claim me as her daughter again. She hopes I'm having a good time? Well I'm not, but what does she care? And if she thinks I'm going to write her back, she can think again.

In the evening I can't keep my mind on the TV, so I get up to go to bed before *Playhouse 90* is over. Aunt June asks me if I'm feeling okay.

"Just a little tired," I tell her.

I'm guessing it's about three o'clock in the morning when I have a bad dream about a dark room of secrets, and I come awake drenched in sweat. I'm breathing too fast, and my heart is flying. At first, I don't know where I am, and when I remember, I don't feel any better.

It's lonely here in the night. The sky is full of stars, but there's no moon. My windows are open to let in the breeze, so I can hear the frogs and the katydids. All the lights are out in the neighborhood, and the cars have stopped running. I could be the last person in the world and not know it. Maybe the Martians came and wiped everybody out. They missed me because I don't belong here. They are looking for me in Elkhorn City.

In the past Mom was always there to comfort me when I had a bad dream, but now she's in Florida having a good time. I look at the mountains dark against the sky, and it comes to me that this narrow valley is like a cradle. It's a comforting thought.

Now, I have to go to the bathroom. I am quiet as I open my door and go down the hallway. Just outside the bathroom a sound comes to my ears, and I can see a light below the stairs. Yeah, somebody's down there.

I fuss about the neighbors being nosy, but I'll have to admit it, I am naturally that way myself. Mom says I get it from her, so I can't help it. I tiptoe to the head of the stairs and listen. I hear a muffled voice—no, two muffled voices. I creep down the stairs. Now I know the sounds are coming from the log room. The door is open and that's where the light is coming from.

I cover more steps, and I am so still I can hear my own heartbeats. Near the bottom of the stairs I bend over the railing, and I can make out two figures in the secret room. One is Aunt June sitting in a rocking chair with an open Bible on her lap. There's a candle burning on a table beside her. There are sure-enough logs in the wall, and a lot of shelves and old furniture. The other person is Emory. He is kneeling on the floor beside her. And he's crying.

At that moment he lifts his face up to her and says, "But what will we do without you?"

And she says nothing, just rubs his hair. He sobs and buries his head in her robe. But I should be ashamed of myself. This is too personal. I should not see this. So I go up the steps even more quietly than I came down. I go to the bathroom and back to bed. I lie there listening, but I don't hear anything.

What will we do without you? What will we do without you?

Is Aunt June going away? Is she coming back? Or is she leaving her family for good? That does not seem likely. But how can I ask about it without giving away that I was on the stairs eavesdropping? Sleep is a long time coming.

8

♪ *This is my Father's world,*
and to my listening ears
all nature sings, and round me rings
the music of the spheres. ♪

Here I am on Sunday morning at the Joy Creek Church of Jesus, listening to some children singing. Aunt June and I are sitting three rows from the back and four from the front of the sanctuary. She is all dressed up, but I'm wearing one of my school dresses, and I don't think she approves of it.

At breakfast, she asked me if this was my best dress.

"Yes, it is," I told her. "It looked a lot better on Mom when it was hers. She had to take it up for me, a tuck here and a tuck there."

That's when I caught Uncle Otis eyeing me, and I felt like crawling under the table. But he surprised me.

"It's a nice-enough dress," he commented, and I nearly choked on my food, "but maybe you should get something fancier for church."

Oh, yeah, sure, I thought, I'll just go right out there and pluck some twenty-dollar bills off that money tree of mine. And what does he know about dresses anyhow?

The voices of the children are as bright as the chrome on Uncle Otis's Plymouth. Aunt June drove us here in it. We traveled deep into the hills for nearly an hour, and finally stopped in front of this tiny pretty white church house beside a babbling creek. Someone was ringing the steeple bell and it echoed through the clear morning into the hills and hollers.

People were hurrying in the door as Aunt June parked the car on the shoulder of the dirt road where a few other cars were parked. But it was apparent that most of these folks walked to the church house. When we went inside, they were already singing a hymn, and everybody stared at us while we found a seat. I could see that my dress was about as "fancy" as some others.

Now the singing is done, and the preacher grins at his congregation like he's so happy to see us he could just bust.

"Praise God!" he says. "'This is my Father's world'!"

"Amen! Amen!" the people say. Aunt June says it too.

It is so hot in here that I am actually fanning myself like an old woman, with a cardboard hand fan I found on our bench. On one side of the fan is a picture of Jesus, and on the other side there's an advertisement— "Crump Funeral Home, for all your bereavement needs since 1904"—and the words to a hymn:

> ♪ *Farther along we'll know more about it,*
> *Farther along we'll understand why;*
> *Cheer up, my brother, live in the sunshine,*
> *We'll understand it all by and by.* ♪

From his Bible, the preacher reads the Sermon on the Mount. Blessed is this, blessed is that.

When he's finished, he says, "Today we're going to invite the Holy Ghost into our humble little chapel. And should he oblige, he might bring his heavenly language with him."

"Amen! Amen!" the people say, and smile and mumble things to each other.

Aunt June leans over and whispers to me, "He's talking about speaking in tongues."

Well, hallelujah! I am thinking. That's sarcastic, I know, but I don't say it aloud. What I wouldn't give to be out there wading in that creek instead of sitting here on this hard bench listening to a hillbilly preacher.

"Now, some people might say we are all cracked!" the preacher says with a glint in his eye.

Again the people react with smiles, nods, and comments.

"And that's something that is not in the Sermon on the Mount, but should be—'Blessed are the cracked, for they are the ones that let in the light!'"

This brings a roar of laughter. Yeah, this preacher is on a roll today. Next comes the sermon. It's not too long—just long enough to put some people to sleep. Then a cherub in a white dress appears out of nowhere—maybe from heaven. Her eyes are china blue, and her hair is as golden as butter. She stands before the congregation, folds her tiny pink hands in front of her, and starts to sing in a voice that pierces the heart.

> ♪ *Soft as the voice of an angel,*
> *breathing a lesson unheard,*
> *hope with its gentle persuasion,*
> *whispers her comforting word.* ♪

When the child ends her song and sits down, people start standing. They also begin to hum and sway with their eyes closed. A whisper ripples through the congregation like a warm breeze. Then this teenager acts like he's been struck by lightning, and falls out. Right beside him a woman with a big old goiter on her neck does the same thing. Both of them are flat on the floor, crying like their hearts are breaking in two, but they are smiling. At first I am startled and wonder if they are all right, but nobody else seems concerned. So I relax and keep watching.

The preacher reads some more scripture in a loud, clear voice. "And suddenly there came a sound from heaven as of a rushing mighty wind, and it filled all the house where they were sitting. And there appeared unto them cloven tongues like as of fire, and it sat upon each of them. And they were all filled with the Holy Ghost, and began to speak with other tongues, as the Spirit gave them utterance. Acts 2:2–4."

No sooner said than done. About five or six people, including the two on the floor, begin to talk in an unknown language—leastways, it's unknown to me. After they have uttered strings and strings of unintelligible words, they seem to run out of steam, and others take up where they left off. The sound of these separate monologues all going on at the same time creates a tuneless chorus of praise to the Lord. Even in the closeness and heat of so many bodies in one place, I think I feel that "rushing mighty wind," as I get chill bumps on my arms. Yeah, this is definitely weird.

I steal a look at Aunt June and see that she is totally spellbound. After what seems like hours, but maybe it's only forty-five minutes, the service breaks up, and the people go back to normal. They start milling around speaking to each other with everyday words, and some people talk to us and welcome us to Joy Creek.

All the way back home Aunt June talks about what we saw.

"Wonder if it's really the Holy Ghost," she says at one point.

"Wonder if he would ever come to me like that," she says at another point.

"Wonder if anybody understands what they're saying."

"Wonder if they're putting on?" I mumble, but I don't think she hears me.

"Look at that!" Aunt June cries as we pull into the yard beside a new blue Chevrolet. "Your poppy's here!"

9

And there he is coming out on the porch. Poppy is tall with a gray mustache and a bald head. He's smiling, and his blue eyes are twinkling as he watches me get out of the car.

When I reach the porch, he says, "Just look at you! As pretty as a spring day."

"Hello, Poppy," I say, and smile up at him.

He takes me into his arms for a big hug, then releases me, but keeps one arm across my shoulders. "I've been watching for you to come home. I couldn't wait to meet you."

We all go inside to the kitchen where Uncle Otis and Emory are reading the Sunday paper.

Emory glances up from the funnies and says, "Well, Princess Garnet, did you get saved?"

But nobody pays him a lick of attention.

We sit around the wooden table and talk while Aunt June cooks Sunday dinner. Mostly it's just me and Poppy talking. Avery chimes in once in a while. Though Uncle Otis and Emory act like they're reading, I know better. They hear every word. Poppy asks me almost the same questions Aunt June asked that first day. He keeps looking at me and grinning.

"A granddaughter!" he says, like he can't believe it. "I have a granddaughter."

And I do some serious wondering. When a man's wife is expecting a baby, it's not something he would simply forget to mention. Could it be that my dad was too ashamed to tell his family he left my mom like that? Well, he should be ashamed.

"Can I call you April?" Poppy asks me.

I know it's the family tradition to be named after the months of the year, but for some reason I feel like if I say yes, I will betray Mom. And even though I am mad at her, I still don't want to do spiteful stuff to her.

"Mom always told folks to call me Garnet," I tell Poppy.

"Okay, Garnet it is!"

I feel he is disappointed, and silence falls over the room for a moment.

"So!" Poppy finally says. "Do you know how your mom and dad met?"

I glance around at the others. They all pretend to be absorbed in what they're doing, but you can almost feel their curiosity. It makes me self-conscious.

I shrug. "Not exactly. At some square dance, I think."

"Down at Pikeville, wadn't it?" Poppy says.

"Yeah," I answer. "I think so. And Mom said he could have charmed the black off a crow."

Poppy and Aunt June laugh.

"She told him a funny joke, didn't she?" Poppy goes on.

"No, it was him told the joke," I say.

"Yeah, that's right. It was August. What was that joke? I don't know if I ever heard it."

Of course I know the joke. I've heard my mom tell it. But now I feel shy about repeating it. What if nobody laughs?

Poppy is persistent. "Didn't your mom ever tell it to you?"

Everybody is looking at me. They expect me to tell that dumb joke.

"Okay," I say with a big sigh, like I'm bored with the whole idea. "This woman rushed in to see her doctor. She was wringing her hands because she was worried sick.

"'Doctor, Doctor,' she says. 'Tell me what's the matter with me. When I woke up this morning, I looked at myself in the mirror and saw that my hair was all wiry and frazzled up, my skin was wrinkled and pasty, my eyes were bloodshot and bugging out, and I had this corpselike look on my face! What's wrong with me, Doctor?'

"And the doctor looks her over for a couple of seconds, then he says in a calm voice, 'Well, I can set your mind at ease on one thing. There's nothing wrong with your eyesight.'"

You might think Jack Benny himself told that joke, the way the kitchen nearly explodes with laughter. Aunt June has to stop mashing the potatoes so she can bend over to catch her breath. Avery and Emory are practically on the floor. Poppy is slapping the table with the palms of his hands, and Uncle Otis? Well, he has tears rolling down his cheeks.

"I'll declare, I'll declare," Aunt June says, and wipes her face on her apron.

"Nothing wrong with your eyesight!" Uncle Otis repeats the punch line, and everybody laughs some more.

"Good one, good one," Poppy says. "That August always could tell a good joke, couldn't he?"

"Yeah, he's the funniest person I know," Aunt June says.

Poppy reaches over and pats my shoulder. "A chip off the old block!" he declares.

Aunt June's dinner of fried chicken, biscuits, mashed potatoes and gravy, green beans, and fresh garden salad is the best meal in the world. Then we have cherry pie right out of the oven, and we eat till our bellies are bulging.

After dinner, we pull chairs out on the front porch and enjoy the day, which is clear and bright. You can hear the birds singing even above the traffic noise.

"Birdy, birdy in the sky," Avery chants. "Why'd you do that in my eye? Listen, birdy, I'm not mad. I'm just glad that cows can't fly."

We laugh some more. I sit right beside Poppy, and every once in a while he touches my hair or pinches my cheek. Lots of people driving around the curve slow down and honk their horns or wave at us, or holler something friendly out their car windows. It looks like everybody knows the Bill family.

The neighbors on either side of the road are on their porches too, and when there's no traffic to drown out their voices, they call things to us. Uncle Otis is usually the one to answer them. Some people drop by and talk to us for a few minutes. Aunt June says they just want to get a look at me. I see Mitzi sitting on a glider between her mom and dad on their porch. Mr. and Mrs. Richards are busy with one customer after another pulling up in front of their store, so we don't see much of them.

After a while a man in a red Ford pickup squeezes his vehicle into the yard alongside Poppy's car. He gets out with a woman and a little girl. It's Uncle Otis's brother, Dewey, his wife, Shirley, and their four-year-old, Madge.

They greet everybody, then tell me hello, heard about you, and that sort of stuff. They are real friendly. There's no more room for chairs, so Aunt June makes Emory and Avery give up their seats for Dewey and Shirley. The boys perch on the edge of the porch with Madge. She is a feisty, pretty thing, and takes a big liking to me. Dewey has a bushy beard like Uncle Otis's, and they tease each other about which one of them is the ugliest.

As evening falls, all of us go into the house to eat leftover chicken for supper. Then Dewey and Shirley say they have to get Madge home and in bed. When they leave, the rest of us watch television. Poppy sits beside me on one of the couches, and we laugh together over every little thing. When the station signs off, Poppy says he is going to sleep in August's old room on the opposite end of the house from the sunporch, and he hugs me good night.

In the yellow room I am surprised to see new shades hanging on all the windows! Now I won't feel so public when I undress.

In my bed I whisper to the darkness, "I must remember to tell Mitzi they can still laugh."

10

"Come on and get up, Garnet."

It's Aunt June standing in the doorway of the sun-porch. I look at her with sleepy eyes.

"What got into you?" I ask. "It's early."

"We're going shopping," she says.

I rub my eyes. Shopping? I've never been shopping in my life. I don't even know how you do it.

"Your uncle and your poppy both gave me money," Aunt June tells me, "and they told me to take you out and buy you some pretty things."

I am speechless. Aunt June smiles at me.

"Just the two of us girls," she says. "You can buy anything you want until we run out of money!"

I am still speechless.

"So get moving."

She closes my door, then pops her head back in again. "Anything within reason," she adds.

"Huh?"

"You can buy anything you want—within reason."

And she leaves the room. I just lie there trying to comprehend. Am I still asleep and dreaming? Money for me from my uncle and my poppy? So, when Uncle Otis said I should get something fancier, he wasn't telling me to go out and pay for it myself. No, he was thinking about footing the bill for me! Then I jump up and dress so fast, I could have my clothes on backwards and my shoes on the wrong feet, but who cares.

When I go to the kitchen, I ask Aunt June, "Where's Poppy?"

"Oh, he went to watch Otis and Dewey make their starting boxes," she said. "They took his car. So we get the Plymouth. Your poppy will drive back home shortly to mind the boys. Now, let's eat and get out of here before Avery wakes up."

Aunt June has fixed a pot of coffee, and I'm surprised when she offers me some. I let her pour me a cup, and I put a lot of milk in it to cut the bitterness. We drink our coffee together, and I feel grown-up. We each have a piece of buttered toast with jelly, then sneak out the front door like we're up to no good.

"Where are we going?" I ask as we head around the curve.

"To Black River. First stop is the Style Corner," she tells me. "They have the latest things for girls. Would you like a poodle skirt?"

"You mean one of those black skirts with the pink poodle on it?"

"That's the one."

"Yeah!"

All the girls at school wear poodle skirts.

"Why did Uncle Otis give you money for me?" I ask Aunt June. "I thought he didn't even like me."

"Of course he likes you!" Aunt June sputters, like I said something ridiculous. "He acts like a big, bad grizzly sometimes, but he's just a teddy bear. It was his idea to buy new things for you. He said, 'Take that girl and buy her a new dress. Nobody living under my roof has to wear hand-me-downs.'"

That makes me squirm. I hate people feeling sorry for me.

"Don't you like having shades on the sunporch?" Aunt June asks me.

"Oh, yeah! I do!"

"You can thank your uncle Otis for that too. He did it while we were at church yesterday morning."

Black River is a bustling town wedged between some big rocky hills. In fact, there are cliffs jutting right down into the street. For a Monday morning in summer it's pretty busy. As we drive along, I see all kinds of stores jumbled together. You could buy anything you wanted here, or go to the movies or go roller skating. There's a bus depot too, a courthouse, and a bank, a post office, and I don't know what all. We pull up to the curb and park in front of the Style Corner. In the window there's a display of red, white, and blue shorts and shirts. Inside, they have air-conditioning, and the clerks all know Aunt June.

I guess they know my daddy too, because they go, "Ooo . . . ahh . . . No foolin'? August's little girl?"

"Ain't she cute?"

Then I get lost in a whirlwind of pretty dresses.

Around one-thirty we take a break at Leon's Burgers. It's a hole-in-the-wall kind of place where they serve nothing but burgers, hot dogs, and pop in a cup over crushed ice. We sit in one of the booths against the window and order cheeseburgers and cherry cokes. Aunt June is in a good mood and starts telling me about growing up in the big green house with my dad.

"We could be as mean as snakes," she is saying, when suddenly my life takes on new meaning and Aunt June fades away.

For there he is, the cutest boy this side of heaven, walking through the door. Near my age, he is wearing a green-and-white-checked shirt, dungarees, and tennis shoes. His skin is tanned, like he spends a lot of time out-of-doors. His eyes are blue. His blond hair is cut in a flattop.

He walks to the counter and perches on one of the stools. He gives his order to the girl behind the counter, then swivels around on the stool, and catches me eyeing him. Rats! I focus on Aunt June, pretending to listen. The waitress brings our burgers. After a few minutes I sneak a peek at him, and rats again! He is sneaking a peek at me!

"I don't think you've heard a word I said," Aunt June says.

I'm startled, but she is smiling.

"It's okay," she says. "He really is cute."

"Who?" I say.

She does not respond but goes on smiling.

We eat our lunch, and I try not to look at the boy on the stool again, but it's not easy. Occasionally I just let my eyes dart around the room. And there he is eating a hot dog like an ordinary person. Aunt June and I finish our burgers and get up to leave. As I follow her out the door, I can feel that he is watching me.

After that, we go to two more stores to shop, and at the end of the day I have a poodle skirt with a blouse to match, three dresses, three pairs of shorts and tops, two pairs of pajamas, some underwear, a pair of sandals and a pair of dress shoes with an inch-high heel, a genuine plastic pocketbook with a poodle on it to match the one on my skirt, and an ankle chain.

On the drive back, Aunt June does not say much. At home, she tells me she is tired and needs to rest before supper, then goes to her room and closes the door.

In the yellow room I spread all my goodies on the bed and dream over them. I see myself going places in these new clothes. One of these years, way, way in the future, like 1980 maybe, when I'm going to seed and feeling blue, I will remember this day . . . and smile.

Aunt June stays in her room, and at suppertime the rest of us sit around the kitchen table, eating pork chops and potatoes that Poppy cooked. He's a good cook—for a man. Says he learned it in the army.

I want to thank Poppy and Uncle Otis for the shopping money, but I don't know how to do it nonchalantly—you know, like it's not an earth-shaking event, though to me it truly is. So it would really be dumb if I were too emotional to get the words out. Or if my voice broke. Yeah, I'll do it some other time.

"Is Mama sick again?" Avery wants to know.

"Yeah, she's feelin' a bit puny," Poppy says.

"Just a headache," Uncle Otis says.

"I think I wore her out," I say. "Shopping is hard work."

I'm trying to be witty, but I guess it rubs Emory the wrong way.

"It's not funny!" he snaps. "Did y'all have to spend the whole dern day tramping around Black River? It was too much for her!"

I'm not only stunned but puzzled at this outburst. Too much for her? It's what I heard Uncle Otis say about me. What are they talking about? It's not like Aunt June's eighty-five. Then I think about how tired she was when we came home, and the memory of that late-night conversation I overheard comes back to me. Is something wrong with Aunt June? Is she going away for her health? I've heard of people going to a better climate when they're sick, but that couldn't be it. Our climate is perfect.

Uncle Otis lays a hand on Emory's shoulder. "She had a good time, son."

Emory lays his fork aside and stares at his plate. I think he is trying not to cry.

The next morning Uncle Otis goes to work as usual, but Poppy stays home with us. Aunt June does not get up, and Poppy says she still is not feeling well. He cooks a late breakfast, or maybe it's an early lunch. I try to help.

In the afternoon I work in the garden again with Avery and Emory. We are hoeing our rows and sweating in the sunshine when Emory suddenly says, "Our old dawg, Roosevelt, is buried right over there." And he points to a spot beside the fence where there is a pile of rocks.

I am surprised Emory is actually making conversation with me, so I encourage him.

"Oh, y'all had a dog?"

But Avery interjects, "He's not there anymore."

We both look at Avery.

"What do you mean he's not there?" Emory asks him. "Of course he's there."

"No, Mama said God took Roosevelt home to be with him."

Emory and I lean on our hoes and look at Avery. His dreamy blue eyes are fixed on a point above the mountains.

"And ever since Mama told me that," Avery goes on in a sad little voice, "I have wondered about something."

"And what's that, Avery?" I say.

"What's God gonna do with a dead dog?"

That's when Emory and I actually laugh together like we've been friends for years. It's a miracle.

On Thursday I get another letter from Mom.

Dear Garnet,

I have a job now selling stuff on the beach. It's not much, but I will find something better by and by. Even so, I will soon have enough money to send for you. You will love the ocean. Please write and tell me what's going on with you. Now, don't you be mad at me, you hear me? Everything will work out. Please write. I love you.

Mom

I toss the letter in the drawer beside my bed with the postcard, and there's the picture of her—the one she packed along with my stationery—smiling up at me. I pick it up and study it for a moment, then lay it facedown and close the drawer.

II

♪ On a hill far away stood an old rugged cross. ♪

I have to admit I enjoy church music. This hymn is
sad and sweet and fills my head with images of a hillside covered with wildflowers long ago and far away.

Aunt June has felt much better these last few days,
and now it's Sunday again, and we are at the Rugged
Cross Chapel at Apple Knob, on the other side of
Black River. This church is built into the side of a hill.
It's larger than Joy Creek. It has other rooms, and it
has bathrooms. The people have better clothes than
the Joy Creek folks, and I'm glad I have a new dress
to wear. It's pink-and-white-pokey-dotted, with a wide
pink sash, and it's the prettiest dress I ever saw, much
less had for my very own. I am also wearing the new

shoes with the baby heels, and my ankle chain sparkles against my skin. I can't quit looking at it.

There's a shortage of hymnals here, so not everybody gets one, including me and Aunt June. But that's okay, because there's a man who looks exactly like Elmer Fudd standing up there in front of us, calling out the words to the hymn. He calls out a line and we sing it. Then he calls out another line and we sing that. It's also a good system for the people who can't read, and I suspect some of these old people can't.

♪ *In that far off sweet forever,*
just beyond the shining river,
when they ring the golden bells for you and me. ♪

This one has a happy sound. And it makes me see children dancing on a riverbank, laughing, their voices like bells in the clear air. When that song ends, Elmer Fudd sits down, and the minister stands up.

"And now we will ask our young people to go through the door to my right here," he says, and points to a door beside the pulpit. "Our youth minister is inside ready to deliver a nice little lesson for you."

Oh, goody, goody, a kiddy sermon.

I roll my eyes at Aunt June, but she gestures that I should go with the other kids. I feel sulky and out of sorts as I follow them. There are maybe thirty of us. On the other side of the door I find myself in a smaller version of the regular sanctuary. I take a seat near a window at the end of a pew. Three giggling girls crowd in beside me.

"Where is he?" one of the girls whispers.

"He's up there beside Douglas," another girl says.

A tall, thin boy around fifteen stands up in front of us and begins to read from the Bible. "And when you pray, you must not be like the hypocrites; for they love to stand and pray in the synagogues and at the street corners, that they may be seen by men. Truly, I say to you, they have their reward. But when you pray, go into your room and shut the door and pray to your Father who is in secret; and your Father who sees in secret will reward you. Matthew 6:5–6."

As he sits down, I notice a door that surely leads to the outside, and I'm ready to bolt. But that thought comes to a screeching halt when I see who is walking to the podium. It's that cute boy I spotted at Leon's Burgers on Monday! Today his shirt and pants are white, and if not for the flattop I would think he is Jesus himself.

"What's the meaning of these verses of scripture?" he asks in a shaky voice.

The girls beside me start giggling again. So this is the person who makes them go mental.

"Jesus tells us that we should go into a private place and shut the door when we pray," he goes on. "That's what my morning message is about."

This is the youth minister? He can't be a day over

fifteen. He has a Yankee accent, and he's obviously not cut out for this. He has stage fright.

"Why does Jesus say this?" the boy asks, then answers his own question. "Because he doesn't want us to be distracted when we're talking to him. He wants us to go inside ourselves and search for answers without trying to impress somebody or worrying about who's looking at us, or what we're wearing . . . and stuff like that."

At this point I think his train of thought derails. His face turns red, and he buries it in his notes. When he looks up again, his eyes meet mine, then dart away, and come back again. I feel a rush of heat come to my face.

"Excuse m-me," he says with a stammer. "I didn't n-notice before, but we have a guest, and we should meet her before we go on."

The girls beside me have stopped their silliness and all three do a slow turn toward me. They stare at me like I have green skin. I study my ankle chain.

"What's your name?" he asks me.

"I'm April Garnet Rose," I say.

He tries to smile, but he's too nervous. "Welcome, April. Would you like to stand up and tell us something about yourself?"

Well, no, I would not. But I do.

"I'm from Elkhorn City, Kentucky, and I'm staying with my aunt June Bill for a while," I say, and sit back down.

Now everybody is staring at me. This is worse than the first day of school.

"Welcome to our church, April. I am Silver Shepherd."

I kid you not. That's what he says—Silver Shepherd.

Then he goes on with his sermon, and after a few minutes he seems to relax and get into it. But I don't hear a thing he says. When he's done preaching, Silver sits down in a chair beside the podium, and the thin boy reads more scripture. I watch the trees against the sky outside the window, trying to seem indifferent to Silver Shepherd. Just because he's about the cutest thing I've ever seen doesn't mean I have to act as silly as these other girls.

After the thin boy closes with a prayer, he says to us, "And now I hope all of you will stay for dinner on the ground, right out yonder on the hillside."

And the youth service breaks up. The door is thrown open and sunshine pours into the room. Everybody goes out into it. This could be the hill in the song that the old rugged cross stood on. It slopes in stages down to the road so that there are level places, where some women have set up folding tables among the flowers and grass.

Now they are placing bowls and platters of food on the tables. I see fried chicken and ham, greens and potato salad, corn bread, biscuits and butter, peas and corn, and I don't know what all. It makes my mouth water just to look at it.

"That's a nice dress, April," someone whispers at my elbow.

I whirl around to find out who it is, and I'm so surprised I can't say anything back. It's Silver Shepherd. He's a few inches taller than me, and up close I can see that his eyes are the color of morning glories.

"Thanks," is all I can think to say. I try to smile, but my mouth has gone so dry, my lips are sticking to my teeth. So now we're both a bundle of nerves.

"I saw you in Black River the other day," he mumbles. I can only nod.

"Do you think you'd like to eat dinner on the ground with me?" he asks, and glances around at the girls who were sitting beside me earlier. They are watching us. "I mean . . . unless . . . you're planning to sit with somebody else."

"Sure. I'd like to," I say quickly. "But I'll have to ask my aunt whenever she comes out."

As more food is piled up on the table, Silver and I just stand there. I think I'm in shock, and he seems to be at a loss for words. After a while the rest of the grownups emerge from the church. I see Aunt June, and she waves to me.

"Be right back," I say to Silver as I sprint to Aunt June.

"Can we stay for dinner on the ground?" I ask breathlessly.

Please. Please. Please. I don't say that out loud, but I think it's obvious to her that I want to stay here more than I want to breathe air.

Aunt June looks into my eyes, then looks at Silver. She smiles and winks at me. "I reckon the men can fend for themselves today. We'll stay."

"Oh, thank you!" I say, clasp her arm briefly, then run back toward Silver.

He is standing there watching me, and I slow down as I draw near.

"She says okay," I tell him.

"Good!" he says.

We fall into silence again, and I search my brain for something to say. Finally, I remember that the weather is a good topic of conversation, so I mention what a nice day it is. Silver agrees. Then he asks if I like school and what grade I'm in. He'll be a sophomore, which is a year ahead of me. Where is my family? He's from Lorain, Ohio, and his dad is a minister. They came to the hills to evangelize, and they are living in a trailer in Black River.

"My dad got the calling to preach three years ago," Silver says, "and that's when he realized that our name—Shepherd—is not just a name but a calling. He says God has called us to be shepherds of lost souls."

"You got the call too?" I ask.

"Yeah, I got the call from Dad."

He smiles at me then, and I smile back. "And how do you like it?"

He looks away toward the hills. "I got mixed feelings about it," he admits.

"So you've been here for three years?"

"No, one year. We were in War, West Virginia, for two years before we came here."

"Was that your dad in the big sanctuary today?"

"No, he does guest ministry at a different place every Sunday. Today he's over in another county."

"Aunt June and I go to a different church every Sunday too," I tell him.

Somebody says grace and we get in line for the food. Silver stands behind me and I can feel his breath on my hair when he talks. Do I like chicken, he wants to know, or ham? Do I like sweets? He had a cat once that loved angel food cake. He called her Angel. Now all the other kids are staring at us like we're Roy Rogers and Dale Evans. It's the first time in my life I have felt like the star of the show. Maybe it's my turn.

"I think April is the coolest name I ever heard," he compliments me.

I don't correct him. He can call me anything he wants.

"No cooler than Silver," I tell him.

His arm brushes mine as we fill our plates. We sit among the wildflowers together, and chat while we pick at our food. I see Aunt June as if she's a memory, floating around over there talking and eating with somebody she knows. She catches my eye and smiles at me, but I am in another place, another time—on a hill far away.

12

♪ *I come to the garden alone,*
while the dew is still on the roses. ♪

I don't know what time it is, but I know it's real early, even for me. I couldn't sleep anymore. My feet are wet as I wander around in the cucumber patch like a girl who is lost and does not care. I love this garden.

There are tiny gossamer webs in the greenery, and when I touch them with my toe they dissolve. A mourning dove is crying somewhere in the misty woods. A thin fog hangs in the hollows between the hills.

"Hidy, Garnet!"

That's Mitzi leaning over the fence, her red curls ablaze. I throw up a hand to her and go over and sit in the grass. On her side she sits too.

"Your hair looks purty in a horse's tail," she tells me. I laugh. "You mean a ponytail."

She is eating again, but today her breakfast does not make me hungry. My appetite left me yesterday. When I finally got food on my plate and sat down with Silver, I couldn't eat. He didn't eat much either.

"I met a boy," I whisper to Mitzi, like there's anybody to hear.

"I know me a bunch of boys," she comes back.

"I mean a cute boy," I tell her. "And he likes me!"

That's when Mitzi lets out this unearthly squeal. But it's okay, I guess, because she goes into such a high register, I think only the neighborhood dogs can hear her.

She has to know all about Silver Shepherd, and I tell her.

"I like him too," I confess to her. "He asked for my phone number."

"Did ja give hit to 'im?"

"I don't know Aunt June's number, but he said he would look it up in the phone book."

"I betcha anythang he'll ast you out on a date," Mitzi says.

"Mom won't let me date," I say. "Aunt June prob'ly won't either. I'll not be fifteen till December."

"Maybe she'll let 'im come to the house and court you."

"Maybe. But his dad's a preacher."

"Preachers ain't no fun," Mitzi says. "This is a sin, that's a sin. You cain't do nothing."

I look toward the sun as it tries to burn away the haze. I love the sun. I love everything today, and everybody.

"I heerd 'bout June being sick," Mitzi interrupts my thoughts.

"She's feeling better," I tell her. "It was nothing serious."

"That's not what I heerd!" Mitzi says. "They say she's got a thang growin' inside 'er."

I am perplexed. "You mean a baby?"

Mitzi laughs. "No, silly. It's something she don't want growin' in there."

All my airy-fairy feelings go poof and fly over the mountaintops.

"Who told you that?" I ask.

"Everybody's sayin' it," Mitzi tells me. "It's the talk goin' around."

Something growing inside her? *What will we do without you?*

I stand up on unsteady legs and see Poppy at the window gesturing for me to come in.

"I gotta go, Mitzi," I tell her, and we say goodbye.

In the kitchen I find Poppy standing at the counter cracking eggs into a bowl.

"Is Aunt June sick?" I ask him.

"No, I think she's just sleeping in," he tells me.

"No, I mean does she have a growth inside her?"

Poppy stops what he's doing and turns to me slowly. "Who told you that?"

"It's the gossip," I tell him. "Is it true?"

Poppy looks out the window at Mitzi and lets out a long sigh.

"Yes, Garnet, and that's one reason I visit as often as I can. I try to help out as much as possible."

"Is she going to die?"

Poppy will not look at me. "The doctors are not sure when . . ." Poppy does not finish that thought. "But we want to make her happy in the time she has left."

I am swallowed up by sadness. I didn't know my feelings could run so high and then so low in such a short time. I don't want to lose Aunt June now that I have found her.

"Oh, Poppy! I've been a burden on her, haven't I?" I go on before he can answer. "That's why Uncle Otis and Emory resented me. They thought it would be too hard on her to have me here."

"They may have thought that at first."

"And now?"

"Everybody sees that you are a blessing, even Otis and Emory."

"A blessing? Really? You're not just saying that?"

"A blessing for sure. June's been more active since you got here. She's started cooking again. It's always been her favorite thing to do. She loves having you go to church with her, and it tickled her good to take you shopping. She always wanted a girl, but . . ."

Poppy does not finish his sentence. He sighs and turns back to his eggs.

"And you know," he goes on, "you have been a blessing to me too."

"How's that, Poppy?"

"Finding you like this when I am just about to lose my only daughter. It's meant the world."

Neither of us speaks for a time. I set the table for two.

"Emory overheard June and Otis talking about it," Poppy continues after a while. "But Avery knows only that she's sick a lot, not that she won't get well. We'll have to tell him eventually, but not yet. And don't let on that you know. She wouldn't like it."

"I won't. I promise."

Emory and Avery don't come down for breakfast, and I'm glad, because I like being alone with Poppy.

While we are cleaning up the kitchen, I say quickly, "Thank you for the shopping money."

"Oh, you're quite welcome," he says. "But most of that money came from your uncle Otis."

"Really?"

"Really," he says, then adds, "Maybe you can help June today. She wants to give herself a Tommy."

"A what?"

"You know, one of those home permanents."

"You mean a Toni."

"I reckon. Toni, Tommy, whatever."

We smile a sad sort of smile at each other.

It's late in the afternoon when Aunt June comes out of her room. She seems in good spirits, and she looks like a teenager dressed in dungarees and a big old shirt that could belong to Uncle Otis. In the kitchen she drinks a glass of iced tea and eats half of a sandwich.

"Poppy says you might need help with your Toni," I say to her with as much pep in my voice as I can muster. "Well, I'm here to tell you, I have a lot of experience with home permanents. Mom never had to perm her hair because it was naturally curly, but I helped Lily with hers all the time."

"Good!" she says. "Let's do it now."

Upstairs we pull a chair into the bathroom and go to work on her hair. She mixes the permanent solution, which stinks to high heaven. We start laughing and cracking jokes as I roll her wet hair around the curlers and tuck the ends into place. We are on the bottom row of curlers when I hear the phone ringing down in the October room, and my heart leaps. Could it be . . . ?

We can hear a deep male voice say, "Hello," and Aunt June says, "I guess Otis is home from work."

I wait. Footsteps coming slow up the stairs. Coming so slow. Hurry, hurry, hurry. I swear to Pete, if he moves any slower, he'll be going backwards.

"June?" It's Uncle Otis's voice.

"Come on in," Aunt June tells him. "We're just putting in a Toni."

Uncle Otis peeps around the edge of the bathroom door, which is partially open.

"I think somebody has a sweetheart," he says, and I feel my face go hot. "And he's on the telephone wanting to speak to Ap-ril."

He draws out the name "April" like it has a dozen syllables in it.

"Is that so?" Aunt June says, and smiles at me in the mirror. "Could it be the boy preacher from the Rugged Cross Chapel?"

"Preacher?" Uncle Otis says.

But I am out of there and down the stairsteps and into the October room where the telephone receiver is apart from its cradle and resting on the forest green couch.

13

*H*ello?" I am breathless.

"Hi there." He's breathless too.

Yeah, it's him. It's Silver. I collapse onto the couch, hug the phone to my ear, and close my eyes.

"It's you."

"Yeah. What are you doing?"

"Nothing. What are you doing?"

"Nothing."

Then silence.

"Say something," he says at last.

"Something," I say.

"Say something else."

"Something else."

We both laugh.

"Okay, I can see," he says, "that I'm going to have to do all the work. What did you do today?"

"I gave Aunt June a permanent."

"A permanent what?"

"A permanent wave in her hair, silly. I bet your mom gets permanents."

He doesn't answer. His mom? He has not mentioned his mom. Wonder why not?

"Where is your mom?" I ask him.

"She's still in Ohio." There's sadness in his voice. "I haven't seen her in a long time."

"Why didn't she come with you?"

"Oh, I don't know. Evangelizing is Dad's thing. Mom doesn't care much about it."

"So, are they separated?"

"I guess you could say that. But not legally. I mean they're still married and all, but . . . What about your dad, April? You told me your mom is working in Florida, but you didn't say a thing about your dad."

"Aunt June is my dad's sister, but nobody seems to know where he is, and I don't care. Mom raised me. But now she's run off too, and dumped me here like a kid dumps a toy when he's through with it."

I bite my lip. I did not mean to say all that, and I hope nobody else heard me.

Silver is quiet for a moment, then he says, "Look on the bright side, April. If your mom hadn't gone to Florida and left you here with your aunt, you and I still wouldn't know each other."

"Yeah, you're right."

Then we talk about everything. We can't put our thoughts into words fast enough. One thing he says is that he would not be in the ministry if his dad didn't insist.

"He thinks I have a gift for it."

"But you don't really like it?"

"No, I don't. But you remember Douglas, the boy who read scripture for me at church yesterday?"

"Yeah, I remember."

"He's on fire to preach. He thinks he's been called by God to do it, and I think that's how you have to feel to be a good minister."

"How did you get the job?" I ask.

"A couple of months ago the deacons called for auditions, and Dad pressured me to try out. I didn't think I would be picked, but I was."

"So I guess they liked you best."

"Yeah, but I don't know why. Douglas is better than me."

I know why. It's because he's cute, and a hit with the kids, especially the girls. But I don't say that.

"You do just fine, Silver, and you'll get better with practice."

"Well, it makes Dad happy, and I don't want to disappoint him."

"You should tell him how you feel."

"You really think so?"

"Yeah, if your heart's not in it, your dad should know."

"You could be right," he says in a slow, thoughtful way.

Somebody comes into the room, and I keep my eyes closed. I don't know who it is. I just wish they'd go away. I want to be alone with Silver.

"Supper's ready, Garnet."

That's Emory's voice. I guess they sent him to get me.

"Who was that?" Silver says.

"My cousin Emory. Supper's ready."

"Oh, okay. Listen, there's a tent revival this week down at Black River. My dad is delivering the message on Wednesday night. Do you think you can make it?"

"Wednesday night? I'll ask Aunt June. She may want to go and take me."

"I'll look for you."

I hang up and turn to the eyes of August Rose on the mantel. And I remember something. When I was a little kid I used to pretend that my dad was somewhere watching me. He would be at the classroom door, or peeping out from behind a tree, or watching from a window in a building or from a parked car—anywhere. Secretly observing.

And when I felt that way, I would show off for him. I would talk louder than usual, and try to say clever things. Or I would sing for him, because back then I actually thought I could sing. Or sometimes I would do a little dance. Or I would run faster than anyone ever ran.

But now I toss my ponytail at him and leave the room. After all, I was only a child back then, and not very smart. I still believed that maybe, just maybe, he cared enough to come back and see me. That's how silly I was.

They are waiting supper for me in the kitchen, quiet and staring as I walk in. I sit down beside Aunt June. She has a plastic cap on her hair while the permanent solution does its work.

Poppy does not care much for the fancy food in the freezer, so he has made us a good hillbilly supper. He slides a pone of corn bread onto a plate and asks, "Do y'all want buttermilk or sweet milk to drink with that?"

We want both, and he brings them out of the Frigidaire to the table. He sits with us, and Aunt June says the blessing. The plates are passed around for soup beans, fried potatoes, and scalded spring lettuce with onions and fat back.

Then Uncle Otis says, "Okay, Garnet, let's have the lowdown on this kid who called. Who are his people?"

"His people? How should I know?" I say.

"Well, do you know if they're Rockefellers, or are they some shiftless clan over on Cripple Creek that runs a still?"

"He's not rich, but I don't know what kind of clan he comes from," I say. "He's from Ohio."

"What's he look like?" is the next question.

"I bet he's got pimples on his face," Emory says.

"He does not! He's cute."

"I'll vouch for that," Aunt June says.

"How old is he?" Avery wants to know.

"Fifteen."

"Well, if you marry him," Poppy says, his eyes twinkling, "can he preach good enough to make a living for you?"

We all laugh. The questions go on, and they listen while I tell them about Silver Shepherd. When the topic of conversation changes, I quietly study these relatives I didn't even know three weeks ago. Yeah, Silver's dad would have to say I come from good people.

When Aunt June starts to clear away the dishes, I say to her, "You just sit there and finish your coffee. I'll clean up the kitchen."

Mom would be proud.

14

I am wearing my new poodle skirt and pink blouse and carrying my poodle pocketbook with nothing in it but a handkerchief and a dollar bill Poppy gave me. I am wearing my hair down and banded with a pink ribbon. I think I am dressed about as nice as anybody else on this Wednesday evening at the Black River tent revival.

I am with Aunt June, Avery, and Emory. I was surprised when those two said they wanted to come. We are under a big tent that is set up on the school playground. We are seated in those folding chairs like you see at a funeral, watching people as they come in talking and laughing. Aunt June, Avery, and Emory know some of the people. Occasionally they wave and smile at this or that one or call out a name.

I don't pay them much attention. I am watching the two tent flaps that serve as doors rise and fall when people come in. Waiting for my first glimpse of Silver. Some little kids keep darting in and out of the flaps. They are tickled with this big old tent, but they are aggravating the tar out of me. Why can't they just sit down or, better yet, go to the playground?

Then there he is. He holds the flap aside and looks for me. He's wearing a red short-sleeved shirt and khaki pants. Our eyes meet, and I am thrilled to see that his face lights up.

"There's your young man," Aunt June says when he comes toward us.

"That's him?" Avery says.

My breath comes in and out of me too fast in little puffs. We say hello and do introductions. Silver speaks to everybody, but he keeps glancing at me self-consciously, and his face is as red as a Christmas bow. Aunt June says something to him, but Emory and Avery are tongue-tied.

"Can I show you something?" Silver asks me. "Outside?"

I look at Aunt June and she nods yes, that it will be okay. We go into the warm summer dusk, and he takes my hand without a word. I know this is a moment that will forever stand out like a shining star compared to ordinary moments. The sky over the mountaintops is navy blue and purple and yellow like a bruise. And the lightning bugs are thick. Somewhere across the river a night bird is crying out his one pitiful refrain— "Whip-poor-will! Whip-poor-will!"

There are people around us, but we don't see them. Some of them speak to us. We mumble something back.

"Over there," Silver says to me, and points to a stack of boxes behind the tent. "There are snakes in those containers. They will be brought out for handling after the service."

"Snakes!" I cry. "Do you handle snakes, Silver?"

"No, I don't."

"What kind of snakes are they?"

"Poisonous ones. Otherwise, there wouldn't be much point. The idea is to demonstrate your trust in God."

Together, we stare at the boxes.

"But I enjoy seeing other people do it," Silver says. "Don't you?"

"I've never seen it done. Are they copperheads?"

"Probably. And possibly a rattler."

"Are they penned up tight so they can't get out?"

"Oh, sure."

"Will you promise me something, Silver?"

"Anything."

"Promise me you won't ever handle poisonous snakes?"

"I promise," he says with a grin. "But that's no

problem for me. I wouldn't pick up any kind of a snake even if you paid me good money."

"So you don't feel like you have to demonstrate your trust in God?"

"Not like that I don't."

We walk around the playground as more and more people go into the big tent, and we are almost alone in the twilight. We don't say anything else. He squeezes my hand so tight, our palms begin to sweat and stick together. We laugh when we pull them apart at the tent flap.

Then, without a word, we go inside with the others. Aunt June has saved two seats for us, and it's a good thing, because the place is packed and some people are standing up behind the back row.

The Black River Baptist Church choir is singing "I'll Fly Away," and on the next hymn we are all invited to join them.

> ♪ *Will there be any stars, any stars in my crown,*
> *When at evening the sun goeth down?*
> *When I wake with the blest in the mansions of rest,*
> *Will there be any stars in my crown?* ♪

Silver's voice is strong, and he hits each note clearly. When we have sung some more hymns, a squatty middle-aged man wearing a pair of thick specs steps up on a raised platform like a stage in the middle of the tent with the audience all around it.

"And now it is my great honor and pleasure," he says, "to introduce to you a most talented man of God— Matthew Shepherd!"

Silver's dad is tall and good-looking, with a neat salt-and-pepper beard. I think I would have known him by his smile. It's Silver's smile. Is this the someday Silver? When he's what? Forty-five maybe? Mr. Shepherd goes to the pulpit in the middle of the stage and begins to speak.

"Welcome, my friends."

It's a sermon full of pleading to all those who have lost their way in life. At one point Mr. Shepherd gets sobs in his voice, and Silver squirms in his chair. The people respond with their Amen's and Hallelujah's. You can tell they like him. He's an interesting talker— I think. No, I'll tell the truth. I don't hear much of what he says. I am still back there under that bruised sky with Silver, and my thoughts are scattered to the wind like dried dandelion fuzz.

But Aunt June is sitting on the edge of her chair, absorbing every word.

After the sermon we sing "Just as I Am" while people pour down the aisle to confess their sins. Mr. Shepherd welcomes each one, says God's blessings are heaped upon them mightily, and arranges for them to be baptized.

"Next Sunday at Hanging Holler," he announces, "there will be all-day activities for young and old alike, plus outdoor preaching, baptism in the river, dinner on the ground, foot-washing, and I don't know what all. We might throw in a wedding or two for good measure."

The people laugh.

And now we get to the real show. Two big, burly men and one short, hefty woman come from the rear, bringing in the boxes of snakes.

"This is Lester, Carl, and Mavis," Mr. Shepherd tells us, "the traveling snake trio from North Carolina. And tonight, my friends, they will show us the power of God."

Mr. Shepherd sits in the audience as Lester, Carl, and Mavis set the boxes down. First Carl goes in for a copperhead and pulls the ugly thing out by its round, fat neck. The people gasp, then ooh . . . ooh and aah . . . aah and clutch each other's arms and hands.

Silver touches my hand.

Emory says, "Dern!" low under his breath.

Aunt June covers her eyes, then peeps between her fingers. Three snakes are out now. One is a rattler. You can hear his old tail going to town. Boy, is he mad. He wriggles and opens his wide mouth, showing fangs. They are real long and sharp, but he does not strike.

The snake handlers put the slithering creatures on

their shoulders and around their necks. That Mavis is just as fearless as the men. She watches her snake with a concentrated look on her face, like she's charming it.

"Glory be to God," Carl says. "He protects his own."

At that Mavis and Lester begin to sing soft and low in harmony.

> ♪ *I sing because I'm happy.*
> *I sing because I'm free.*
> *For His eye is on the sparrow,*
> *and I know He watches me!* ♪

"Amen!" the people say. "Amen."

"His eye is on the sparrow!"

"Hallelujah!"

Yeah, it's a show worth watching all right. Directly, the snakes are put away, and everybody breathes a sigh of relief. Nobody panicked and nobody was bitten. It's a miracle. Mr. Shepherd dismisses us with prayer, and the service closes. I am sorry it is over, for now Silver and I have to go our separate ways. First he introduces me to his dad, but Mr. Shepherd is so busy shaking hands, he barely has time to give me more than a nod and a pat on the back.

"God bless you," he says, then turns to somebody else.

Silver walks us to our car and tells us all good night.

Aunt June and Emory sit in front, me and Avery in the back.

"Wonder if I could do that?" Aunt June is pondering things out loud again on the way home. "Wonder if I would have enough faith in God?"

"Wouldn't try it myself," Emory says.

"Naw!" Aunt June says, and laughs. "Me either."

A pale yellow moon, more than half-full, has come up over the hills. It peeps out from behind the scattered clouds and sees me. I smile. Hello, there, Moon, my old friend. Yeah, it's me, April Garnet Rose. It's still me even after all that's happened.

"You know what I wish?" Aunt June says to nobody in particular.

And nobody answers her.

"I wish they'd have a faith healer at one of these things. That's what I wish."

"A what?" Avery asks.

"A faith healer. You know, it's a preacher that heals people through faith in God."

"Heals them from what?" Avery wants to know.

"From whatever ails them," Aunt June says. "A cold, maybe a sore throat, a bellyache."

"Or question-itis," Emory says as he glances back at his little brother. "You got a bad case of that."

Emory's eyes meet mine for a moment. Then he looks out at the moon over the mountaintop.

15

On Thursday, just like clockwork, there's another letter from Mom.

> Dear Garnet,
>   I don't know why you won't write me back.
> I've been looking every day for a letter from
> you. You are the most hardheaded girl I
> ever saw. Write to me. You hear me? You're
> not too big to whip, you know, so don't
> make me come up there.
>   I am working hard every day, and saving
> all my money for you.
>
>   Love, Mom

"Not too big to whip!" I say to Silver that night on the phone. "Like she's in the habit of whipping me.

Why, she never did whip me in my life! And I'll tell her one thing, she better not start now."

Silver does not say anything.

"Are you still there?" I say.

"Yes," he says. "I'm just listening."

"I'm not writing to her," I say stubbornly.

"But it seems like she's worried about you, April."

"What if she is? It serves her right for dumping me like she did."

We are both quiet.

I am the first to break the silence. "Say something."

"Something," he comes back.

"Say something else."

"Something else."

It's not funny anymore.

"I took your advice, April," he says. "I told Dad how I feel about the ministry."

"You did?"

"Yeah, and I told him I want to quit."

"What did he say?"

"He argued with me, but I stood my ground, and after a while he gave in. Then he said he'd pray for me. That's what he says when he's disappointed in me."

"But he'll get over it, won't he?"

"I suppose. But anyway, I took your advice, now you have to take mine."

"And what advice do you have for me, Silver?"

"I think you should tell your mom that you are mad at her, and tell her she hurt your feelings."

I sigh. "So you think I should write to her?"

"Yeah. She's your mom, and she's worried."

"Do you write to your mom?"

He is silent.

"Well, do you?"

"Sometimes," he mumbles.

"I'll think about it," I tell him.

"As soon as Dad agreed that I don't have to preach anymore," Silver goes on, "I called Douglas and asked him to fill in for me until they can get another youth minister. He's happy to do it, and I imagine the folks at Rugged Cross will want him full-time. That means I will be free on Sunday morning. Are you going to the all-day thing at Hanging Holler?"

"Yes!"

"Good. I'll meet you there!"

I go into the television room and find Uncle Otis reading the newspaper. I am still bashful around him. It's been more than a week since I got all those new clothes, and I have not had the nerve to thank him. He probably thinks I'm thoughtless and rude. Maybe now?

"Hey, Uncle Otis."

"Hey." He glances up. "Was that your beau on the phone?"

"Yeah," I say. "It was Silver."

"Well, you know, Garnet, I was saying to your aunt this morning, how nice it is having a teenager in the house."

This is a surprise. I wait for more, but he pretends to be absorbed in the paper.

"Thanks," I say to him, then add quickly before I lose my nerve, "and thanks for the clothes money. I never had pretty things before."

He mutters something, but still does not look up. Could it be he doesn't know what to say next? Then it comes to me that adults don't always know how to act either, same as kids. I guess we're all just muddling through, making mistakes, but doing the best we can. I sit there for a moment, then get up to leave the room so he can read his paper in peace.

16

♪ *Oh, come to the church in the wildwood,*
oh, come to the church in the vale.
No spot is so dear to my childhood
as the little brown church in the vale. ♪

Here we are at the morning service in this pretty little church at Hanging Holler. It's made of brown stone and sits close to the Dismal River. I am sitting between Silver and Aunt June. Silver's dad is up front with six other preachers.

Just before the sermon, the little cherub who sang at Joy Creek appears out of nowhere, walks to the front of all those people, and starts singing "It Is No Secret." Silver whispers to me that her name is Denise, and she is famous in these parts. She goes from church to church singing at a different place every week.

It's a regular service, with hymns and prayers and preaching—no speaking in tongues, and no snake-handling. Then we all go outside into the sunshine, where once again I find myself sitting with Silver on the grass eating dinner on the ground. Only this time we actually eat.

Aunt June sits with us, and after dinner she starts chatting with some people she knows. So Silver and I walk on a path through a wooded area by the river. There are other young people all around us.

"Your grandfather's name is January," Silver says to me, "your aunt's name is June, your dad's name is August, and you are April."

"Right."

"If you ever have a kid of your own someday, would you name it for a month?"

"I don't know. I reckon you could name a girl May."

"March would be a cool name for a boy," he says.

"And speaking of names," I say, "how did you get yours?"

"From the Lone Ranger's horse, natur'ly!"

"Truth or lie?"

"Lie," he confesses. "My mom's name is Goldie, and when I was born, my dad said to everybody, 'Now I have all the gold and all the silver I will ever want.'"

There is sadness in his voice and in his face.

"Why would your mom let you go so far away from

her, Silver?" I ask. "I can tell you miss her, and she must miss you too."

He doesn't answer.

"Sorry," I mumble. "I didn't mean to pry."

"It's okay," he says softly. "Naturally, you're curious. I . . . I can't really talk about it right now, but . . ."

"That's all right. You don't have to talk about it."

"But I will tell you all about her eventually," he says. "I promise. Just not today."

We come to a tree with smooth gray bark and Silver takes a small knife from his pocket. He carves S.S. + A.R. I watch as he carves the heart. When he is finished, we just stand there admiring it. I am wondering how many years it will remain there. Distant singing breaks the silence.

♪ *Shall we gather at the river,*
where bright angel feet have trod,
with its crystal tide forever
flowing by the throne of God? ♪

The baptism service is beginning at a wide place in the river below the church. Silver takes my hand, and we walk that way with the other young people. Those who are to be baptized look like a painting, as they sit there, dressed in white robes, on the green riverbank with their ministers. The singers are standing behind them, and the other people are gathering around to watch.

Mr. Shepherd has more immersions to do than all the other preachers put together. The sun throws sparkles on the moving water as he leads his first sinner in. She is a pretty woman with dark glossy curly hair. As she wades, the water makes her white robe rise and bob around her, and she has to push it down. Mr. Shepherd lifts his hands to the blue sky and shouts into the clear afternoon air, "I baptize you, Maria Beth Bartley, in the name of the Father, the Son, and the Holy Spirit. Amen."

Then, with help from another man, he ducks Maria Beth Bartley all the way under the water and brings her up again. And she is saved. I am not sure from what. Hell, I reckon. But I don't know about that hell stuff. Would a real honest-to-god God allow such a thing? The woman sputters, then smiles through tears. She is helped up the riverbank by friends and family. The people shout Amen and Hallelujah, and Glory be to God.

After the baptisms, the foot-washing begins, and I've never seen anything like it. This is where you show your humbleness by taking a bucket of water and bathing somebody else's feet. It's what a woman did for Jesus in the Bible.

The grownups don't invite the kids to join in,

probably because they know we would make a big joke of it. That's what Silver and I are doing anyway. We are trying not to laugh—well, not right in people's faces anyhow—but we have the silly giggles and can't help ourselves.

When we see Silver's dad starting to wash this old fat man's feet, we whisper things about stinky toe jam and dirty toenails and stuff like that until we are in stitches. But suddenly Mr. Shepherd catches Silver's eye and gives him a look that would melt a lump of coal. I watch Silver's face go red and serious, and we don't laugh anymore.

The next event of the day is outdoor preaching. You can hear it going on everywhere—by the riverbank, in the woods, in the churchyard. People get into little bunches around their favorite preacher, and encourage him with their Amen's and Hallelujah's. Silver's dad's flock is behind the church, flanked by blackberry bushes in full bloom. Aunt June is with that group, and we go and sit in the grass beside her.

Mr. Shepherd's voice is like music as he talks to his followers about Jesus. I watch the river moving through the valley between the green mountains. What a glorious day! I could never have imagined that this summer among strangers would turn out so fine for me. I begin to daydream about me and Silver. Maybe we could go to school together this fall. Maybe I'll ask Mom to let me stay here while she works and saves her money—but no. I look over at Aunt June and float sadly back to earth. *What will we do without you?*

Mr. Shepherd's voice is a hum, blending in with all the other hums and buzzes of summer. I have no idea what he's talking about until all of a sudden his words pierce through the other sounds.

"Someone is in pain. I feel it," Mr. Shepherd is saying. His eyes are closed, and he is clutching his Bible so hard his knuckles are white. "Someone has a disease and needs the healing power of Jesus."

Aunt June rises to her feet and says something I can't make out. Everybody looks at her.

Mr. Shepherd opens his eyes and holds out one hand to her. She moves toward him like she's underwater. I feel my scalp prickling, and the little blond hairs on my arms come to attention like tiny electrical wires.

"And he healed all who were sick." Mr. Shepherd is quoting scripture as he takes Aunt June's hand. "This was to fulfill what was spoken by the prophet Isaiah, 'He took our infirmities and bore our diseases.'"

"I believe," Aunt June says. "I believe."

"What is your name, my dear lady?"

"June Bill."

"And what is your sickness, June Bill?"

"I have a cancer growing in me." Aunt June's voice

is thin and trembly. "It is eating away my life, and I don't want to leave my family yet."

"Do you believe that God can heal you of this cancer?"

"Yes!" she cries, and clasps her hands to her heart. "Yes, I believe."

Then Mr. Shepherd asks his congregation if they believe, and everybody says Yes, or Hallelujah, or Glory be to God. I find myself nodding my head slightly. Yes? I believe?

"Pray!" Mr. Shepherd tells us. "Everybody pray!"

He lays one hand on Aunt June's head, closes his eyes, and calls out in a loud voice, "I command all disease to leave this body of June Bill. In the name of Jesus, I command it now! Heal!"

Aunt June immediately crumbles to the ground like all her bones have turned to Jell-O. The people are rising to their feet, some shouting, some applauding, some breaking into song. All of them gather around Aunt June, touching her, hugging her.

Aunt June weeps. "I am healed!" she says. "I can feel it. My body is whole."

I don't know how to feel or how to act. Part of me wants to cry and hug Aunt June and tell her I'm happy for her. Another part of me wants to slink away and pretend I don't know her or any of these people.

"It's a miracle," the people say.

"God has performed a miracle."

Mr. Shepherd says to Aunt June, "Go! Be it done to you as you have believed."

I look at Silver and wonder what he thinks about this. His expression does not tell me. Without a word, the two of us turn and drift away from the others and walk down the woods path.

"I didn't know she was sick," he says after a while.

"I just found out recently," I tell him. "Does your dad do a lot of healings?"

"He has never done one before—that I know of."

We continue our walk in silence, thinking about what we saw and heard back there. I am confused. I think Silver is too.

The day begins to dwindle into evening, and everybody gathers around a bonfire at the river's edge. Some women bring out hot dogs and marshmallows, and we toast them while we sing spiritual songs.

Aunt June is the topic of conversation and the center of attention, and she is so happy. I finally go to her and hug her.

She hugs me back and says, "Garnet, you have witnessed a miracle this day."

I don't know how to reply, so I lie. "I didn't know you were sick."

"I didn't want you to know," she says, "but now it doesn't matter. I am healed."

Finally we call it a night and go to our cars.

"I'll call you," Silver whispers close to my ear, and we have to go our separate ways.

"What a day!" Aunt June exclaims as we pull away from the church.

"I guess you're exhausted?" I ask her.

"No, I never felt better in my life!"

I wait for her to talk about what has happened to her, but she is uncommonly silent all the way home, and I am glad. Because I don't think I can handle any more God stuff today. My head is spinning.

When we get home we can hear the television. We go in there where Uncle Otis, Poppy, Emory, and Avery are watching *What's My Line?*

"Guess what, Garnet!" Avery says. "Your mom called from Florida!"

"Mom called?"

"Yeah," Uncle Otis says. "We had a nice chat together. She's going to start a new job in two weeks. It's in a hotel, and they are giving her a room for the two of you. She also has the money for your bus trip to Daytona Beach. She's sending it to you."

"When?"

"A few days."

I am stunned.

"She wants you to call her and work out the details. Here's her number."

I stare at the piece of paper he hands to me with a phone number written on it. Leave here now? Leave this house? Leave Silver?

"She said to call as soon as you get in."

"Tonight?" I say.

"Yeah, tonight."

"Do you know how to make a long-distance call?" Emory asks me.

I look at him and see that he's not being a smart aleck. He's merely asking.

"You dial the operator," Aunt June says, "then tell her what city you are calling, and give her that number."

"I'll do it later," I say as I leave the room.

"She's waiting by her phone," Uncle Otis hollers after me.

Well, she can wait till the cows come home. And then some!

17

♪ *The chimes of time ring out the news,*
another day is through.
Someone slipped and fell.
Was that someone you? ♪

It is Denise's angelic voice in my head when I wake up
from a troubled sleep. All my windows are open and
the shades rolled, to let in the cool night air. It's almost
like daylight in here, because that partial moon I saw
on Wednesday night is now full.

I sit up and look out the window. The grocery store
is shut tight. Next door Mitzi's window is dark. In fact,
I see no lights anywhere. The mountains are silhou-
etted against the night sky. I am in a cradle. I belong
here. I am safe and happy. And for the first time in my
life I am like everybody else.

Then I see movement in the garden, and it's like a TV show begins to unfold before me. Someone is walking in the moonlight, and an awful wave of sadness washes over me. I know who is here to haunt me. It's a little girl in a tattered dress. And she is crying.

Everybody in her class saw the holes in her socks during exercise period. They laughed at her and teased her.

"Darn it, Garnet! Darn it, Garnet!" they yelled.

"That was a hard day," I whisper to the little girl.

Then someone else is moving through the dew behind the child. She is the mother. She has fried potatoes for supper. It's the only thing in the house to eat. Worse yet, the mother has a bad cold. She can't swallow without pain, and her head is stopped up. But still she has to get up in the morning and go to work.

"You have always done your best," I whisper to the mother.

And I know in my heart it's true. Everything she does is for her child.

"Give your mother a hug," I whisper to the girl. "She loves you so much."

But the little girl floats into an apple tree and disappears. The mother stands alone in the garden and turns her head toward the sunporch. She stretches out one hand to me, and I see the sadness in her eyes.

From my nightstand, I clutch the paper with the telephone number on it, and stumble from bed. I open my door and peep into the hallway. All is quiet except for Uncle Otis's snoring. Barefooted, I tiptoe down the stairsteps and enter the October room. I can almost read the number in the moonlight, but not quite. My fingers are shaking as I turn on the lamp beside the telephone and dial the O.

"Operator."

"Daytona Beach, Florida," I tell her, then give her the number. After about nine rings a gruff male voice answers.

"Yeah?"

"Who is this?" I ask.

"Who is this?" the man comes back.

"I need to speak to Betty Rose," I say.

"Who?"

"Betty Rose. She called me from this number earlier tonight."

"This is a pay phone, kid, on a street corner, and I was just walking by."

"A pay phone?"

"Yeah, a pay phone. You know—a phone you put nickels in."

"I know what a pay phone is, but . . ."

"You know what time it is?" the man says.

"No."

"It's two-thirty in the morning."

A nameless, faceless voice in the night, telling me that it's late—too late.

"But you're still up," I say stupidly.

We are both quiet for a moment, then the man says, "Anything else, kid?"

"No, thanks."

I hang up and stand there staring at the phone. Then I turn to the mantel and look at my daddy.

"Why did we think she had her own phone?" I say to him. "She's never had one in her life. It would be nice, wouldn't it, if for once she could have a nice convenient thing like that? It's not much to ask for, is it?"

My father's smile seems to mock me.

"What are you grinning at?" I say to him. "You deserted her first!"

The night is quiet as a tomb.

"Now she has nobody."

I go back to the yellow room and turn on the lamp beside my bed. I open my nightstand drawer, take out the package of stationery Mom packed for me, then find a pen, and write a letter to my mother.

Dear Mom,
    I am so sorry I did not call you. I've been
mad at you, and I guess you know why.
But I'm not mad anymore. I'm having a
good time here at Aunt June's, but I want
you to send the money to me for the bus,
because I do want to be with you more than

anything. I have so much to tell you. I love
you and miss you.

Your loving daughter, April Garnet Rose
XXXOOOXXXOOO FOREVER!

I address the envelope to the last address Mom
gave me. Surely, if she moves, she will check back
there for mail. Then I place a stamp in the upper right-
hand corner. I will ask Uncle Otis to mail it for me
tomorrow.

I turn off my light and slip between the sheets.

"I will make it up to you, Mom," I whisper to the night.

Yes, I know what I will be leaving behind. I will miss
Silver most of all. But I'll miss Aunt June too, and
Poppy, and sweet little Avery. I'll also miss Mitzi, and
Uncle Otis and Emory, even this puke green house. It's
like a live character in my drama. I always knew, didn't
I? Yeah, I knew it was not forever. It was temporary. But
once I began to like it here, I acted like this was my real
home, and it's not. Wherever Mom is, that's home, and
that's where I belong.

18

It's Wednesday morning, and I'm just lying here in the bed, looking at the sky. I think it's going to rain, and it will be the first time since Decoration Day when I got here. I have not told Silver yet that I'm leaving soon, but I'll probably tell him today. I haven't heard from Mom again.

I can hear movement somewhere in the house, and I wonder if Aunt June is up. She has a doctor's appointment today. She is convinced that she's healed, but Uncle Otis and Poppy told her they don't much believe in faith healing, and I saw them looking at each other with troubled eyes behind her back. Aunt June said she will believe whatever the doctor says. Then she smiled this mysterious smile. Could she really be healed?

I told Poppy about the late-night phone call to Mom,

and he fussed at me for not calling when I was supposed to. He said it was a thoughtless thing to do, and he's right. He left to go to his house on Monday evening. He said he had some business to attend to in Bluefield, but promised to be back here this evening.

"Don't you go to Daytona Beach while I'm gone," he said to me.

I promised I wouldn't.

Last night Aunt June sat Avery down and had a long talk with him about her sickness and her healing.

He listened with big eyes, then said, "I wish we would have knowed Silver's daddy when old Roosevelt got sick. He might have made him better."

"Maybe so," Aunt June said with a smile, and hugged him.

She has been so full of energy and resolve these past two days, she's about to work me to death. She has gone into a cleaning frenzy, which I have felt obliged to help with. Then she recruited Emory and Avery—against their will—to pitch in. We have cleaned every nook and cranny in this old house, and the porches and the yard on top of that. I'm almost afraid to get up now and see what she has for us to do today.

At one point during our dirt purge I overheard Emory referring to the sunporch as "Garnet's room." No room has ever before been called Garnet's room. I wonder what the hotel will be like where I will be living with Mom.

Finally I roll out of bed. I go to the bathroom and take a bath and dress in a pair of my new shorts and a matching top. I pull my hair back in a ponytail and go barefooted down the stairs. I think I will have some cornflakes for breakfast. Silver says he eats cornflakes every day.

But as I am about to go in the kitchen I stop short and let out a little gasp, because I see a strange man peering inside Aunt June's Frigidaire. My first thought is that this man just walked in off the highway, and now he's going to steal our food. I mean, nobody ever locks an outside door around here.

"What do you want?" I say in the meanest tone I can manage.

At the sound of my voice, he pulls his head out of the Frigidaire and turns to face me. He has the wildest, blondest beard I ever saw, and it grows ever whichaway.

"Well," he says to me. "Who might you be?"

I put my hands on my hips and try to look stern. "Never mind who I am. Who are you and what do you want?"

That's when he gives me this grin, like he does not take me seriously at all.

"Feisty one, aren't you?" he teases me.

He closes the Frigidaire, sits down at the table, and crosses his arms, like he's settling in for a while.

"Who are you?" I repeat.

"I asked first," he says, still grinning.

I am beginning to lose my nerve. "I'm warning you, my uncle has a gun. So you had best be on your way."

The smile fades as a flicker of confusion crosses his face. "Your uncle?"

"That's right. My name is April Garnet Rose, and my aunt and uncle own this house."

"Ap-ril . . . ?"

Now it looks like he's lost his nerve too.

"April Garnet?"

"Yeah, that's right. April Garnet Rose."

Something is going on now with his expression, but with all that bushy hair on his face, it's hard to say what.

"Where did you get that name?"

"Where do you think? My mother gave it to me."

"Who . . . ?" It seems he can't get his words out, and now I can see what's happened with his face. It has gone ghostly pale. "Who is your mother?" he croaks.

"Betty Rose."

He sits perfectly still while he stares a hole through me. He does not move a finger or an eyelid. He's like a statue. And a thought comes to me. No, it couldn't be him, could it?

"Now it's your turn," I say, and my voice trembles a bit. "Who are you?"

But he does not answer my question.

"How old are you?" he asks, with so much serious-ness it's scary.

I am rattled, but I answer him. "I'm fourteen, but I'll be fifteen in December."

"December?" he croaks again. "What year were you born?"

"Nineteen forty-two."

He goes on staring at me. And now I can see it in his eyes. They are my eyes. They are the eyes in the photo on the mantel. It was the beard that threw me off.

"I'm August Rose," he says.

I don't recognize these feelings that charge through me. They are all so different and some of them hurt, and some of them feel good, and some of them are mean, and wild as a wolf.

So I run. Through the dining room, past the log room, up the stairsteps, and into the safety of Garnet's room, where I curl up in a tight ball on my bed.

19

*M*aybe a half hour passes, and there's a knock at my door. I stay still. The door opens.

"Garnet," Aunt June says.

I don't answer.

"I know you're not asleep," she says.

I hear rain.

"Garnet, you should talk to him."

I don't move, and I hear her closing my windows.

"He really wants to talk to you."

Go away. Go away. I don't say it out loud. I would never say that to Aunt June. But she does go away. I hear the door closing softly. I hear pattering against my windows. Outside the air is cooling. The mountains are rejoicing with the summer rain.

After a while I get up and look out the front window.

There's a brand-new white '57 Chevy in the yard beside the porch. And it's a convertible. Well, lah-de-dah. It must belong to him—the Happy Wanderer, Aunt June calls him. I reckon he just wandered in this morning, from God knows where, and soon he'll wander away again. But I don't care.

I pull my vanity chair to the back window and look at the rain. It's good for the garden, but we'll have to weed again real soon. There's another knock on my door. I don't move. The door opens. I don't look around but I know it's him.

"April," he says.

"Garnet!" I correct him sharply. "Mom always calls me Garnet, and now I know why."

"And why . . . is that?" he says uncertainly.

"Because the month names were the Rose family tradition, and she was mad at you."

"Oh. All right then—Garnet. Will you talk to me?"

"You deserted us," I say.

"I did not know about you," he says, and I hear him sitting down on my bed.

I finally turn to face him. "How could you *not* know?"

"I left in April, 1942. At that point, she probably didn't know herself."

I am more than a little stunned. He didn't know? All of these feelings—the hurting ones, the good ones, the wild ones—are fighting each other inside me.

"April Garnet is the name we picked out in the event we ever had a girl," he says. "When you told me your name, I knew the truth. And I never even suspected before that moment. I swear."

Could this be true? He didn't know that I was expected? Why would Mom lead me to believe he knew? That he walked out on both of us?

"And what about a b-boy?" I stammer.

"What?"

"What would y'all have named a boy?"

"Oh." He smiles a little. "August Second."

He wants me to think that's cute, but I don't.

"Where have you been?" I snap, sounding like Mom used to sound when I came in from playing too late.

"Everywhere, but the last six months I was in Bristol working." He touches his face. "I don't usually look like this. I heard about the centennial celebration, so I grew this beard before coming back. I hate it."

"Me too. Why don't you shave it off?"

"I will on the Fourth of July, along with everybody else."

I can't believe it. Here I am talking to my father for the first time in my life, and what's the subject? His beard.

"How long are you staying?" I ask.

"Indefinitely," he says. "I'm thinking of coming back here to live and work."

"Mom and I are going to live in Florida," I say real quick.

"So I hear," he says.

I turn back to the window and watch the rain.

"Garnet," he says.

But I don't answer.

"Garnet, I don't blame you for being hurt and angry."

"Who says I'm hurt and angry?"

"You do. You say it with every move, every word you say, and every word you don't say."

I shrug.

"Do you think your mother will let me come and visit you in Florida?"

I don't respond.

I hear him sigh. "Garnet, now that I know I have a daughter, do you think I can forget about you? I'm sure I've missed a lot, and now I want to be a part of your life."

"Mom and I have been doing extremely well, thank you very much, without you."

I cross my fingers, because that was a whopper.

"Will you tell me about it?" he asks.

"About what?"

"About growing up. What it was like. I want to know you."

"No."

He is quiet, and I'd like to turn around and see his

expression, but I can't look into his eyes again. They are warm eyes, and I know that's how he fooled Mom for so long—with his deceitful warm eyes. Maybe he didn't know about me, but he deserted her!

"I have been all over the South," he says. "From the oil fields of Texas to the cotton fields of Georgia. I've been to the Ozarks and the Smokeys, the sand hills of South Carolina, and the bayous of Louisiana. From Virginia Beach to Miami Beach."

"Well, I've never been anywhere, except to come here!"

"That's too bad," he says sympathetically, but then he goes right on talking. "I think I liked the ocean almost as much as the mountains. Can I tell you a little story?"

I don't say yes or no.

"It was one night maybe a year ago. I was sitting in my car in Virginia Beach."

He acts like I have agreed to hear his story.

"I was watching the ocean waves rise and fall, rise and fall. There was a full moon and about a zillion stars. And suddenly I had this overwhelming sense of loneliness come over me. I guess I was feeling sorry for myself."

In all my thoughts of August Rose, I never did imagine him feeling sad.

"I finally fell asleep," he goes on. "I often sleep in my car. And in my dream I could hear the roar of the ocean. I was walking on the beach at the end of the world at the end of time. There was nobody left but me."

I finally turn around again to look at my daddy, and his eyes don't leave my face as he continues his story.

"Then above the roar of the ocean, I clearly heard my own voice saying, 'Go home.'"

He is quiet for a long time, and I don't interrupt his thoughts.

"I woke up alone on an empty beach in the early morning hours," he said, "but that experience haunted me, Garnet, and you know what I think now?"

"What?" I say almost breathlessly.

"I think the dream was calling me back here, maybe because of you."

My eyes are stinging, but I won't cry! I'm not a pushover for sentimental stuff.

"On the conscious level, I didn't even know about you, but maybe, just maybe, on some other level I did know. Understand?"

"Yeah, I do. But why did it take you a whole year to get back here?"

"I had some work obligations," he says, "but I'm here now."

Again we sit in silence. Then he leans forward and grins at me.

"And what kind of welcome do I get? A wild girl threatens me with a gun!"

He reminds me of Poppy now, and I can't help smiling.

"You look like your mom," he says. "I don't know why I didn't see that right off. She was the prettiest girl I ever saw."

"She's still pretty," I say as I go to the drawer and produce the snapshot of her. Proudly, I present it to my dad.

I watch his expression as he studies Mom's face. Something flickers there in his blue eyes, but I can't quite read him yet. Then without commenting, he tucks the photo into his shirt pocket. I start to tell him I want the picture back, but for some reason I don't.

I sit down again in my vanity chair.

"I'll bet she never told you that she ran me off," he says.

"Who? Mom?"

"Yeah, she told me to pack my things and get out. She never wanted to see me again—but I'll admit I was relieved."

"Well, she says you ran away with a carnival singer."

"That was not true."

"Mom never lied to me."

"I'm sure she didn't. She told you what she believed to be true. But she was wrong."

He does not look away as he tells me this. I heard on the radio one time that when someone is lying to you they can't look you straight in the eye.

"I met that carnival singer and I joked around with her a bit and teased her. I guess some people would call it flirting. But my only purpose was to get free tickets for Betty and me to the carnival."

"And Mom quit you for that?"

"Yes and no. It got all blown up out of proportion and turned into a big ugly thing. It was the last straw, you know, in a long list of . . . stuff."

"Stuff?" I say. "Did you do that kind of stuff all the time?"

"No. Once I met Betty, there was nobody else. She just couldn't take my word for that. She was too insecure."

"What do you mean?"

"Well, I guess you know that when she was five or six years old, her mother died. Her dad dropped her off at the house of a distant relative and never came back for her. She couldn't believe that I would not leave her too."

The shock of Dad's words renders me speechless for a moment. No, I didn't know that about Mom. She would never talk about her childhood.

Her dad dropped her off at the house of a distant relative and never came back for her? But no, it was too cruel. So cruel I can't even let it enter my head that she planned the same fate for me.

"And I did leave her," Dad goes on. "We just couldn't get along. It was at the point that I was ready to leave, and when she told me to get out, well I did."

"If y'all really loved each other," I say, "it seems to me like you would have tried to work things out."

"First of all, we were both hot-tempered and hard-headed."

Hardheaded? That's what Mom called me in her last letter.

"And second we were just kids—and really dumb," Dad says.

"Hot-tempered and hardheaded does not sound like Mom."

"I reckon she's grown up, and so have I," Dad says.

"She's done her best by me," I tell him.

"I'm sure of it," Dad says.

20

Now we are at the kitchen table and Aunt June is making her special recipe pancakes and sausage. She has poured coffee for us, and I sip at it, liking it better than I did the first time.

Dad can't get enough of staring and grinning at me, the way Poppy did that Sunday when we met. I guess I do my share of staring and grinning too.

Aunt June places an arm across Dad's shoulder and kisses him on the head. Her cheeks are glowing and her eyes are shining. In fact, she strongly resembles a person who is healthy as a horse. She and Dad obviously had a talk this morning during the time I was cowering in my room after meeting him in the kitchen, so I wonder if she told him then that she has been healed of cancer.

"I've missed you, big sister," he says to her.

"Now tell the truth, you missed my cooking!" she teases him.

"Yeah, especially your cooking."

Aunt June places a pitcher of cold milk, a crock of hot syrup, and a mound of butter on the table, then serves up the pancakes and sausage. She joins us at the table, and we feast.

The rest of the day is hectic. First, Emory and Avery come down to breakfast, and they are both tickled pink to see their uncle August. Later Uncle Otis comes home to take Aunt June to the doctor, and then Poppy comes home from his trip to Bluefield, and there's a lot of hugging and backslapping.

Around five o'clock I manage to slip away from everybody and go to the October room to wait for Silver to call, which he does, and I can't get the words out fast enough. Of course I tell him about Dad first.

"And you're not mad at him anymore?" Silver asks.

"No. He didn't know about me. How could I be mad?"

Then I tell him about Mom calling, and that I will be leaving for Florida soon.

"How soon?" he wants to know.

"I'm not sure. I'm hoping Mom will give me some more time to visit with my dad."

"And what about me?"

Is Silver feeling left out?

"I want to see you as much as I can," I assure him. "But when do you think we can get together again?"

"I'm not sure. I'll ask Dad."

I'm thinking it would be cool if his dad brought him up here. Then I tell Silver about the second important event of the day.

"Now, this is really, really weird," I warn him.

"Yeah? Well, tell me something weird, April Rose."

"Aunt June went to the doctor, and he could not find a sign of the tumor that was growing in her—not even a trace. It's gone."

"Hmm-mm" is all that Silver says.

"Don't you think it's peculiar?"

"Dad will be overjoyed to hear it," Silver says.

"How do you explain it, Silver?"

"I can't really, but maybe it's like those firewalkers in India when they place their bare feet on hot coals and don't get burned."

"I've heard of that."

"Well, it's something like that. They do it with their minds. It's a simple case of mind over matter."

What an evening we have in the big friendly kitchen, with its gigantic fireplace, leather sitting area, and its dozen chairs around the wooden table! We are celebrating Aunt June's healing and Dad's arrival and our first day together. I am sitting between Aunt June and

Dad on the couch. Old friends drop by to chat, to reminisce, to laugh. And to every single one of those people, Dad presents me proudly as his daughter.

"Can you believe it?" he says.

Or, "I never dreamed."

Or, "Isn't she beautiful?"

Through all this, there is music—of sorts—pouring from the kitchen radio, because my dad wants it on, no matter how disturbing the racket. Uncle Otis's brother, Dewey, and his family are here; Mr. Richards has left his store to pop in for a moment; and a black-faced coal miner who went to school with Dad has stopped by on his way home from work.

The room has become a dictionary picture beside the word "chaos" when Aunt June can stand the hysterical singing on the radio no longer. She throws up her hands, yells, "Eee-gads!," slaps the radio knob to Off, and sits back down.

Thunderous silence falls over the room for only a moment; then the laughter and talking erupt even louder than before.

"That's the spirit you've been missing, my girl," Poppy says to her. "That's my spunky girl."

Aunt June grins.

"August, hanging around you and your people is still as much fun as ever," the coal miner says. "Got any new jokes for us?"

"Speaking of jokes," Uncle Otis interrupts, "this girl of yours, August, can tell a good one."

All eyes turn to me, and I feel my face go warm with the praise and attention.

"Well, tell one then!" Dad says to me.

But I feel shy. "I can't think of one right now."

"I got one! I got one!" Avery cries out. He is on the floor with Madge, helping her color a page in her Mouseketeers coloring book.

"Oh, Avery, your jokes are dumb," Emory says.

"Well, jokes are supposed to be dumb!" Dad says, and smiles at Avery. "Tell it, partner."

"Okay." Avery stands up and tells his joke, like he's as big as anybody. "These two cannibals are eating a clown, and one cannibal turns to the other and says, 'Does this taste funny to you?'"

We all laugh heartily at Avery's "dumb" joke, and he beams.

"Now it's your turn, August," Poppy encourages him.

"Okay," Dad says, and looks around the room at his audience. "I heard this one in Mobile, Alabama. A woman gets on a bus with her baby, and the bus driver says, 'Lady, that's the ugliest baby I've ever seen. Ugh!'

"And the woman, fuming, goes to the rear of the bus and sits down. She says to the man next to her, 'That driver just insulted me!' And the man says to her, 'Well, you go right up there and give him a piece of your mind. Go ahead, and I'll hold your monkey for you.'"

As everybody laughs, I look around at all these happy faces and think about how my life has changed in such a short time, how much I love it here in this house beside the road with all its joyful people.

And I realize it's always been just me and Mom getting by with no male persons in our life at all. Now, I have not only a daddy and a grandpa, but also an uncle and two boy cousins. And of course, there's Silver! My heart aches now for Mom, who, except for me, has been alone forever and a day. As all this goes through my mind, I admit that I really would like to stay here forever, but how could I leave my mom? First Dad, and then me? No, it would break her heart. And I would definitely miss her.

It seems I can't have it all, no matter which way I look at it. So I shrug away the thought and get back to this precious moment. The television is forgotten as we carry on far into the night. When we finally are ready to turn in, Emory and Avery double up so that Poppy can have Avery's room and Dad can have his old room back.

At the top of the stairs my dad wraps his strong arms around me and whispers, "I love you, Rosebud."

I am almost overwhelmed, but I manage to say, "I love you too."

21

Silver calls while we are eating lunch the next day. It's an odd hour for him to phone, and his voice flutters like a shaky leaf in the wind.

"I have something important to tell you."

"How important?"

"Important enough that I don't want to tell you on the phone. I'm trying to get Dad to bring me up there to see you."

"Great! When?"

"I'm not sure. Whenever he has time to drive me."

"Well, I need to know. With Dad here, it's—"

"I know!" he interrupts me. "I know your dad is there, and your life is suddenly all peaches and cream!"

I am too surprised to reply.

"I'm sorry, April," he mutters. "I'm so sorry. I don't

know what's wrong with me. Well, I do know, but . . . but . . . I mean, I shouldn't take it out on you."

"What is it, Silver? Has something happened?"

"I'll explain everything when I see you."

"Okay. Just let me know when you can come."

We try to make light conversation then, but it's no use. We say goodbye and hang up.

When I go back into the kitchen, I get the feeling that Aunt June and Dad have been discussing me. Aunt June has probably told him about Silver. Now they are quiet.

I sit down to my grilled cheese sandwich, but it's cold, and I'm feeling uneasy about Silver. What could be wrong?

"Well, who is he?" Dad asks me. "Will I ever get to meet him?"

"Maybe, if you behave," I tease him. "Or maybe not."

"Does your mom allow you to have boyfriends?"

"I've never had one before," I tell him.

"Well, I think fourteen is a bit young."

"We don't date!" I protest. "We've only been together at church."

And he says no more.

It's Saturday evening when Mr. Shepherd brings Silver to see me. In his royal blue shirt and dungarees, he looks very handsome. Everyone is in the kitchen as usual, and I am so proud to bring Silver in to meet my dad. After introductions, Aunt June and Mr. Shepherd start babbling excitedly about the healing, and I pull Silver away so that we can be alone. I lead him into the October room where we sit side by side on the forest green couch.

Silver looks at the telephone on a table beside us. "So this is where you talk to me on the phone?"

"The very place."

"This is a nice room."

"Yeah, I love this room."

I don't know what else to say. I wait for Silver to speak, but he seems far away from me, and he avoids my eyes. Aunt June sees Mr. Shepherd to the front door, and they pop in to speak as they pass.

"I'll come back for you at ten, Silver," Mr. Shepherd says.

Then he leaves, and Aunt June returns to the others. After that, we can hear the traffic and vague murmurings from the kitchen. The rest of the house is quiet. Silver squirms and glances around the room. He looks at his feet. He scratches behind his ear.

"What's wrong, Silver?" I say softly.

"It's about my mom," he blurts out.

"Your mom?"

"Yeah. I need to tell you about her."

I don't say anything. I just listen.

"She's been in an institution for the last three years. She has schizophrenia."

"What's that?"

"It's a mental illness." His voice is barely a whisper now.

I don't know how to respond because I don't know anything about mental illness.

"It's like she's not my mom anymore," he says sadly. "She doesn't even look the same, and the last time I saw her she thought I was somebody else."

"That's awful, Silver."

"Do you still feel the same about me?" he asks.

"Of course I do!" I touch his arm. "Why wouldn't I?"

He shrugs. "Well, I was only a kid when she started getting sick and we tried to care for her at home. That was hard, because sometimes the other kids saw her then wouldn't play with me. I guess they thought schizophrenia was contagious, and they might catch it." He leans back on the couch and rubs his eyes with the backs of his hands. "And sometimes they made fun of me. They called me names."

"I've been made fun of. I've been called names," I tell him. "It hurts."

"And there's more," he goes on.

I brace myself.

"Dad thinks he has healed your aunt. I keep telling him that he really didn't have much to do with it. Your aunt healed herself with the power of the mind. But then he preaches to me that I don't have enough faith in him. Now he believes he can heal anybody, and he wants to go back home and heal Mom."

"Back to Ohio?"

"Yeah. It's like he's obsessed now. It's all he can think of."

"So y'all are leaving?"

"Yeah."

"How soon?"

"Tomorrow."

"Tomorrow!"

"Afraid so. We're already packed. Dad has to do a wedding at two o'clock. It's something he committed to months ago. It's over in Kentucky, and we will go on to Ohio from there."

I am stunned. Tomorrow? Silver will be leaving me tomorrow?

We hear laughter from the kitchen.

"I think sometimes Dad is crazier than Mom."

"What do you mean?"

"When Mom had to go away to the hospital, he was inconsolable, so I felt like I lost both of them. He couldn't accept that she would never get better. That's when he got religion and thought God was talking to him."

"And what did God say to him?" I ask.

"To come here and preach to the people of Appalachia."

"Why here?"

Silver shrugs again. "I don't know. Maybe Dad thought people here needed him more because so many of them are poor. He didn't ask me what I wanted, and I really hated this place right up until the day I met you. Then I started to love it, and now I want to stay at least as long as you are here."

He takes my hand and looks into my eyes. "You will probably be gone to Florida when—and if—we come back, but I want to write to you. Will you write back?"

"Of course. I don't know yet what my address will be, but you can send a letter here in care of Uncle Otis. Aunt June will send it on to me."

He puts a hand into his shirt pocket. "I have a present for you."

He places a small box in my hands. I open it quickly and find a gold locket on a pink ribbon.

"Oh, Silver, it's beautiful," I say to him. And it really is. I have never had such a pretty piece of jewelry.

"It opens up," he says.

But I have already found the tiny catch that springs the heart open. Inside there are the usual openings for two photos, facing each other. In one of them is a picture of Silver.

"It's just a school picture," he says. "I thought you might want to put your own picture in the other side, and we will be face to face over your heart."

"Oh, yes, I will," I say. "I love it, Silver."

I position the ribbon around my neck and he ties it for me.

"And can I have a picture of you, April?"

"Mom has all my pictures with her. But I'll send you one as soon as I can."

A little before ten o'clock, we walk out on the porch together, and he kisses me for the first time. It's a sweet quick kiss, but then he pulls me close to him.

"When I am old enough to make my own decisions, April," he whispers into my hair, and his voice breaks a little bit. "I . . . I will come to you. I will find you wherever you are. I promise."

I don't trust my voice to answer him.

"Unless . . ." he goes on, "unless when the time comes, you don't want me anymore."

"Of course I will still want you, Silver!"

"I will miss you every day," he whispers so softly I almost don't hear him.

We are standing apart, facing each other with the fingers of both our hands intertwined, when Mr. Shepherd pulls his car into the yard. Without another word, Silver goes to the car and gets in. I can barely make out his face in the dark. He throws up one hand to me. Then I watch the red taillights of his dad's car disappear around the bend. And Silver is gone.

22

When I go inside I find that Uncle Otis, Poppy, Emory, and Avery have gone to the TV room to watch *Gunsmoke*, but Aunt June and Dad are in the log room. I peep in the door, hoping to be invited in, and I am.

"Come on," Aunt June says. "I know you're curious about this room."

I enter and look around at the heavy, dark furniture and all the books.

Aunt June is sitting in the rocker, which is the only place in the room to sit, and Dad is leaning against a bookcase, going through an old photo album.

"Is your boyfriend gone?" Dad asks.

"Yeah," I say. "He's gone for good."

"Preacher Shepherd told us," Aunt June said.

Both of them are studying my face, looking for signs of tears, I reckon.

"I'm okay," I say. "We're going to stay in touch. He's going to send the first letter here, Aunt June. Will you send it on to me when you have my address?"

"Of course."

"There will be lots of boys, honey," Dad says sympathetically, "because you're a cutie."

I lean against the bookcase beside my dad. "There will never be another Silver," I say sadly.

"That's true," Aunt June says.

Mom is the only other person I would ever share these feelings with—and maybe Mitzi. So I'm thinking how good it is to have somebody to talk to, when Dad has to spoil it all by saying, "This is how it will go. You will write to each other often for the first few months, and pretty soon you'll forget his face, and before you can count the days he's been gone, you'll have another boyfriend. I'm telling you, Garnet—"

"I have his picture," I interrupt, more than a little irritated, and open up the locket for them to see.

Both of them glance at the picture of Silver in the locket and make no comment.

"But life goes on," Dad continues.

"Absolutely," Aunt June agrees, "and I promise you, Garnet, the pain you are feeling now will pass."

"That's right," Dad says, and places an arm around me. "You'll be amazed how quickly it will pass."

"And how soon did you get over Mom?" I say, looking up at him.

He is obviously caught off guard. He glances at Aunt June. She has a slight smile on her face. He changes positions against the bookcase, pulls his arm away from me, and folds both arms across his chest. Aunt June and I wait silently and watch his face.

"That was different," he finally says. "It was a more serious relationship. We were older, and we were married."

"You're still married," I remind him, "but you didn't answer my question."

He doesn't know what to say, and there is silence in the log room for some time.

"Y'all think because I'm a kid, I don't feel things deeply?" I say at last.

"No, I don't think that at all," Dad says.

"Me either," Aunt June agrees. "I think sometimes kids feel things even more deeply than adults."

"I'm sorry," Dad says, "if that's how we came across to you."

"He said he will find me again someday," I say, and my voice trembles. "And he said he will miss me every day."

Aunt June and Dad look at each other and have the good sense not to say anything else about time, and forgetting Silver's face, and finding a new boyfriend. Dad puts his arm around me again.

"I'm sorry," he repeats. "I'm sorry about everything."

I think of the happiness we've shared for the last few days, and suddenly I want to put away all this sad stuff on a high shelf in my brain and pull it down later when I'm alone. So I change the subject.

"How do you feel, Aunt June?"

"I feel absolutely wonderful."

"Silver says that you healed yourself with the power of your mind," I tell her. "He says it's something like the people in India who walk on hot coals and don't get burned. They do it with their minds."

"That's an interesting theory," Dad says.

"Except that I didn't do anything," Aunt June says. "I just opened up my heart and my mind to the possibility of being healed, and I felt all this electricity shooting through me."

"Did it hurt?" I ask.

"No, not at all." She laughs a little. "It didn't feel like a shock. It was just a surge of energy. It was amazing."

"Are you sure you had cancer?" Dad asks her.

"I only know that I was very sick and in a lot of pain, and three different doctors told me I had a malignant tumor, and they all agreed it would kill me. Since my healing I have had no pain, no sickness. In fact, I have never felt better in my life. And the same doctors who told me I was going to die now say there is nothing wrong with me."

"Wow!" I say. "So Silver's dad actually did it."

"No, Garnet, Silver's dad is only a person like you and me, with no special powers," Aunt June says. "He simply provides the conditions for a healing to take place."

"What conditions?"

"The ceremony, the prayers, the expectations."

"Maybe he's the conduit through which the electric current flows," Dad the electrician interjects.

"Something like that," she says. "But I think we all have the power to heal ourselves without help from another person, if we believe and keep our minds open."

"Did you read that in one of your books?" Dad asks her, gesturing around at the shelves.

"Yeah, there are lots of good ones in here," Aunt June says.

"So why do you keep this room locked?" I ask her. "Maybe somebody else would like to come in here and see your God stuff, as Avery calls it."

"You are welcome to do that," Aunt June answers me with a smile. "Just ask me, and I will unlock it for you. There are also valuables hidden in here, in the drawers, in the bookcases, even in the floor. Old diaries and photographs, family heirlooms, insurance policies, tax papers, rare books, even money."

I glance around the room. The history of the Roses, I am thinking. Yes, before I leave I will come in here and snoop.

"So I guess you did find God?" I ask her.

"Yes, I found him."

"At Hanging Holler?" I ask. "Or at Joy Creek? At Apple Knob?"

"No, I found him here," she says, and touches her heart. "He was here all along, closer than breath."

Closer than breath. I touch my own heart and feel its beat and think about my breath moving in and out of my lungs.

"There is nothing outside us that is going to save us," Aunt June continues. "The kingdom of God is within."

23

$\mathcal{E}$arly the next morning Mitzi and I are sitting in the grass as the sun burns away the mist and chill of the night.

"Lost love can be found again," she says to me, and these are the most hopeful words I have heard since Silver left. Yes, he did promise to find me again.

"Thanks, Mitzi. You know how to make a person feel better."

"Where y'all goin' to worship at this morning?"

"I'm not going. I'm spending the day with Dad because I don't know how many more days I will have with him. Aunt June is trying to decide now where she will become a member. Today she's going to a church up at Garden Branch, where they're going to do some shouting."

"Some what?"

"Yeah, according to Aunt June, they get the Holy Ghost and start shouting. It's part of their worship."

"You tell me some right innersting stuff, Garnet. I'll be sorry when you're gone."

"Yeah, me too, Mitzi. I guess I'll be leaving as soon as Mom sends me the money for the bus."

"I'm gonna miss you bad, Garnet."

"I'll miss you too, Mitzi. I'll write to you. Will you write me back?"

Mitzi hangs her head and mumbles, "I cain't read and write."

Of course she can't. I knew that. And now I've embarrassed her.

"That's okay, I'll still write," I say quickly. "Your mom can read it to you."

"Yeah!" she says, and her pudgy face seems to bloom with the sudden joy of that realization. "And she can answer fer me too. I never got no letter before. How quick kin you write me once?"

"Give me time. I'm not even gone yet!"

And we laugh together in the sweet morning dew.

In the afternoon Dad takes me and Emory and Avery to Black River to see a movie. It's *The Night of the Hunter* with Robert Mitchum and Shelley Winters. It's real suspenseful, with this haunting music that hangs around like a spirit long after the movie is over. But even better than the movie is the ride in Dad's convertible. I get to sit up front with him while Emory and Avery sit in the back.

On the way home, Dad talks about his work as an electrician. "It has made it possible for me to travel as I wanted to," he says. "I can get a good job anywhere in the country doing what I love."

"Then you can move to Daytona Beach," I say to him, "and get a good job down there close to where I will be living with Mom."

"I doubt that your mom will want me to do that."

"But she can't stop you."

"Maybe she'll let you come up here and spend the summers or something like that—if I don't antagonize her."

"What do you mean?"

"I mean if I make her mad, she may not let me see you."

I think about that for a moment, then I say emphatically, "No, Dad. Mom's not spiteful like that."

"She's not?"

"No, she's real sweet and good-natured."

"Then can you explain why she has kept you from me all these years?"

I can't answer that, but I feel like I have to defend her. "She's been the best mom in the world, and I miss her."

Later, when we return home, I come up behind Dad sitting at the picnic table in the backyard. I can see that he is studying the snapshot of Mom, and his face is sad.

Suddenly I hear in my head, Lost love can be found again!

I stop dead in my tracks, then slip away before Dad knows I am there.

I manage to keep my mind off Silver almost all day long. But when darkness comes I think of him and wonder how far he has traveled today with his dad. They were not leaving until after that two o'clock wedding. Would they be in Lorain, Ohio, yet? Probably not. Sleep is a long time coming for me.

24

*B*y Monday afternoon, I'm beginning to wonder why I have not received the money from Mom. I'm on the front porch writing another letter to her, a long one this time.

Dad wanted to get a look at Uncle Otis's business, so a little while ago he rode with Poppy up to the shop. The boys are playing in the backyard, and Aunt June is in the kitchen starting supper.

I gaze at the mountains, trying to find the right words to tell Mom about Silver. A long Greyhound bus comes around the curve and screeches to a stop in front of Richards' Grocery. I am so absorbed in my letter I am not paying much attention to who is getting off that bus, until suddenly there she is—Mom!

As the bus moves on, she looks with uncertainty

toward the house. She seems so small standing there beside the road holding a suitcase.

"Mom!" I yell, and drop everything where it is.

She sees me and smiles and waves.

I run to the edge of the road and stop, because this is a road you do not rush into, no matter who is on the other side waiting for you. Mom sets the suitcase down. When all is clear I run across and straight into her arms.

"Oh, Mom! Mom! I have missed you so much, and I'm so sorry!"

"No, I'm the one who's sorry," she says as she hugs me tight. How good it feels to be in her arms again.

We are both crying and hugging and talking at the same time.

"I should have called you that night. I'm sorry I didn't."

"I'm sorry I left you here to fend for yourself among strangers!" Mom says. "I knew how hurt you were when you didn't write, or call me back that night."

"No, it's okay. I've had a big old time. These are good people."

"I know they are. Otherwise, I couldn't have left you here."

Mr. and Mrs. Richards both come outside the store to see what they can see. About the same time Mrs. Mays comes out onto her porch.

I grab Mom's suitcase and nudge her across the road before they can detain us.

"I'm actually glad now," I try to reassure her, "that you brought me here. It's been fun."

"That's good, but I'm here to fetch you," she says with a smile.

We reach the porch.

"Mom, you didn't have to go to so much trouble and expense. I did write to you the day after you called. I told you to send me the money for the bus. Didn't you get my letter?"

"No, I got nothing from you, but no matter. I'm here now. I borrowed money from Grace to come up here before I start my new job, and this way you don't have to ride that bus all the way to Florida by yourself."

Now I ask her the big burning question. "Why did you let me believe that Dad knew about me?"

She is absolutely quiet, and she won't look me in the eye. I'm puzzled that she doesn't answer. Did my mom lie to me after all?

"Did you hear me?"

"Yes, I heard you, and I don't have a good enough answer for you."

"But, Mom! All these years I have believed my dad knew I was expected, and that he didn't want to see me, that he didn't even care if I was a girl or boy."

"I wanted to get back at him," she says so softly I can

hardly hear her. "He didn't deserve to know you, and I didn't want to share you. And I was so angry and hurt when I found out that he ran off with that . . . that person."

"But he didn't! He didn't!"

"Of course he did . . . but—" she interrupts herself. "What do you know about it?"

"I've met him," I tell her.

"No kidding?" she says, then looks at the front door. "Is he here now?"

"He's not inside right this minute, but he'll be back soon. He came home a few days after you called."

And now I can't read my mom. I thought I knew her every expression. But the look on her face is one I have never seen before. And I can tell she is shaken.

I try to calm her. "He's been real nice to me."

She covers her face with her hands. "I should go, Garnet."

"Go where? What are you afraid of?"

Aunt June comes out wiping her hands on her apron.

"I thought I heard someone out here," she says, then exclaims, "I'll declare! I'll declare!"

"It's Mom," I say.

"It sure as the world is!" Aunt June cries. "What a nice surprise."

"Hello, June," Mom says. "I came on the Greyhound to get Garnet."

I carry the suitcase for Mom as we go inside.

"Come on in the kitchen and have a glass of iced tea," Aunt June says to Mom. "You must be worn out. How many hours were you on that bus?"

"Too many," Mom says. "But I'm not going to put you out. I can find a place to stay tonight. And we'll get the first bus we can catch tomorrow."

"Nonsense!" Aunt June says. "You'll stay right here. You can sleep with Garnet. Your bed is big enough for two, isn't it, Garnet?"

"Oh, yeah, it's plenty big," I say.

We leave the suitcase in the hallway and go into the kitchen for tea. Although Aunt June is well into cooking supper, she insists on fixing Mom some crackers and cheese for right now with her tea. Mom accepts the snacks gratefully. She has not eaten since breakfast. I can't wait to tell her about Silver, so I do it while she's eating. She seems surprised, and her mind is taken off Dad for a few minutes.

"My little girl," she exclaims. "How grown-up you are! When did it happen? And look at your clothes! Where did you get that pretty outfit?"

I tell her about Poppy and Uncle Otis pitching in to buy me new things. She doesn't say a word about that, and I wonder if it makes her feel bad that somebody else had to buy me clothes.

Then I hear car doors slam, and I know it must be Dad and Poppy coming home. I decide I'll just go warn

Dad that Mom is here so it won't be such a shock when he sees her. I run through the dining room to find him coming in the front door.

"Hey, Rosebud!" he says to me. "Is this your stuff out here on the porch?"

He's referring to my letter-writing material.

"Yeah, but, Dad, listen . . ."

"You better pick it up before the wind gets it."

Poppy enters and barges right on to the kitchen. Dad starts to follow him, but I clutch his arm.

"Dad!"

"What? What is it?"

"Mom's in there, Dad."

"In there?" He points toward the kitchen like he does not believe me.

"Yeah."

"Right now?" he croaks.

He looks at the suitcase sitting in the hallway, and I watch his face go pale again as it did on the morning when he first realized who I was.

"Yeah, she just got here on the Greyhound bus, and she's nervous to see you again, so be nice to her."

He stares at me blankly, but he does not go toward the kitchen again. He rubs one hand across the back of his neck. He turns toward the door as if to leave. I can almost see his mind racing. Then he looks at the stairs, and bolts up them two at a time.

25

In the kitchen Poppy and Aunt June are being very attentive to Mom, trying to put her at ease, but in spite of all their efforts, Mom seems agitated and uncomfortable again. I sit down beside her.

"I told Dad you are here."

I watch Mom's fingers flutter to her throat. She takes a long, deep breath.

Aunt June is working as fast as she can on supper, and Poppy pitches in to help. They try to keep up a steady stream of conversation as they work together, but nobody mentions Dad. I keep watching the door, expecting him to come in at any time, but he does not appear.

After a while, the boys come in from the backyard and Uncle Otis arrives home from work. They are all very pleasant to Mom, and Avery tells her she is prettier than Shelley Winters.

When food is placed on the table, Dad still has not appeared, and Mom says uneasily, "I think maybe I'll just go and rest for a while. I'm not very hungry anymore."

"Oh, no, Mom," I protest. "Please eat supper with us. We have so much fun at meals."

"Oh, yes, we do," Poppy says. "You don't want to miss a meal at this table."

"Garnet, go find your dad, and tell him supper is ready," Aunt June says.

I go slowly through the dining room and up the stairs. Dad's bedroom door is open but he's not in there. I hear water running in the bathroom, so I tap on that door.

"Dad?"

No answer.

I tap again. "Dad?"

He mumbles something.

"Dad, Aunt June sent me to fetch you for supper."

"Oh. Okay."

I wait for a moment, then ask him, "Are you coming down?"

"Yeah. In a minute."

I go to the front porch and collect my letter-writing stuff, then wait for Dad at the foot of the stairs, but he does not emerge. I go back to the kitchen.

"He said in a minute," I tell Aunt June.

I sit beside Mom and touch her hand. She tries to smile at me. When everybody is seated and there's nothing left to do but wait for Dad, silence falls over the kitchen. Then we hear him on the stairs, and I breathe a sigh of relief.

"Oh, there he is," Aunt June says, and I can tell she is relieved too.

When I first see Dad walk into the kitchen, I am thunderstruck. You can tell he has showered, as his hair is all wet, and he has changed into fresh clothes, but the shocker is that he has shaved off that wild beard, and now you can see the bare handsome face from the photo on the mantel. There are a few razor knicks on his neck, but other than that, he has come through his brush-clearing bloodless.

Of course everybody is staring at him with open mouths, but to my relief nobody mentions that he has shaved.

"Betty," Dad says politely to Mom, and nods his head in her direction.

"August," she replies just as politely.

Dad sits down across from me and Mom, and Aunt June says the blessing. As the food is passed around, the tension melts a little for the rest of us, and we begin to eat and talk all at once, but Mom and Dad are quiet as they peck nervously at their food. They don't look at each other or exchange comments at all.

I realize this supper is not as much fun as I told Mom it would be, and when we're done eating, everybody lapses into silence again. It's just too weird for words, and I start thinking ahead. How will it be with Mom and Dad here in the kitchen for the after-supper get-together? Will we still have laughter? Or will the mood be spoiled? But Mom has been on a bus for hours. She will probably want to go to bed early. And tomorrow? My spirits sink. Yes, early tomorrow we'll be gone from here, maybe forever.

Then Dad startles me right out of my thoughts.

"You should have told me!" he exclaims. And it's clear that he's talking to Mom and nobody else.

"Told you what?" Mom replies, although everybody, including her, knows exactly what he means.

"About Garnet. I could have helped."

Mom's face is scarlet, but she manages to answer calmly. "We got along just fine." And I'm thinking now it's her turn to cross her fingers. "Besides, you were not there to tell, remember? And I didn't know where you were."

"You could have contacted June," he says.

"Well, I did contact someone—your old buddy, Jake," Mom says, "and he informed me that you left town with Brenda."

"Brenda who?" Dad sputters.

"You know who!" Mom sputters back. "The carnival singer!"

"I never knew her name," Dad says. "I told you then and I'll tell you again, there was nothing between me and that carnival singer. But that Jake Farmer!" Dad laughs a funny bitter laugh. "Jake was in love with you! Of course he wanted you to think I ran away with that girl. He figured with me out of the picture, he might . . ."

Dad pauses and looks around the room at all the faces watching him and listening, and he suddenly appears embarrassed and self-conscious.

"Go on," Uncle Otis says to him, like he can't wait to hear what's coming next.

"Well, I did hitch a ride with the carnival because, if you'll remember, I didn't have a car," Dad continues, "but I didn't see that singer again a'tall. I was with—I don't know how many people, scrunched up in the cab of a truck. I rode all the way to Louisville holding a redheaded midget on my lap!"

Small explosions escape from Emory's mouth, and he covers his face with his hands. That's when all my nervous tension bubbles to the surface, and I fight back my own giggles. To hide a smile, Uncle Otis acts like he's picking something up off the floor. But Mom is not smiling, nor is Dad.

"I turned eighteen the day we got to Louisville, so I joined the army and went to war," Dad goes on.

"Eighteen!" I cry. "So how old were you when you got married?"

Dad and Mom glance at me, but neither one answers.

"They were both seventeen," Poppy volunteers. "I had to sign for them."

"Only three years older than I am right now!" I say. "And, Dad, you think I'm too young to—"

"Anyway," Dad interrupts me. "I was sent overseas." He clears his throat and changes positions. "You knew where I was when you got my allotment checks, didn't you?"

"Yes," Mom says, "you were about as far away from me and Garnet as you could get—across the ocean."

Dad clears his throat again and goes on. "After a year, I was wounded and sent home."

"Yeah, he got shot in the butt!" Avery explains.

That's just too much. Emory and I lose it.

But Dad seems rattled, and Mom's face looks like it might crumble.

"I'll declare," Aunt June says. "Aren't we being rude? Here y'all are trying to have a serious conversation, and all we can do is laugh. August! Betty! Come with me right now!"

She gets up and starts out of the room, then turns and motions for Mom and Dad to follow her. They both protest mildly, but Aunt June will not take no for an answer.

"Come on now, right this way," she says.

They follow Aunt June from the room, and I follow at a distance. She leads Mom and Dad to the log room, opens the door, which magically seems not to be locked for once, and motions them inside.

"Now, y'all go in there and talk it all out," she says kindly. "Nobody will bother you."

Reluctantly Mom and Dad go into the log room together, and Aunt June shuts the door behind them.

26

Aunt June shoos me back into the kitchen where she puts an arm around me and says, "They have a lot to work out in private."

For the next half hour we hear an occasional muffled outburst, but mostly there is no sound from the log room. We begin, one by one, to wander into the TV room. When it's time for pop and candy I get up to go to the store with Avery.

"Y'all be careful crossing that road," Aunt June hollers her usual reminder.

In the hallway I tiptoe to the door of the log room and place my ear to the crack beside the latch. Avery comes up beside me as we both listen.

I hear Mom saying, "You know as well as I do there are no jobs here for women. Men get all the breaks."

I can't make out Dad's reply. When Avery and I get back from the store, I take drinks and candy to Mom and Dad. First I listen outside the door again. I don't hear anything. I knock.

"Come in," Dad says.

I go in. They are standing across the room from each other.

"I brought you some treats," I say, and set them on the table beside the rocker, along with a bottle opener.

They say nothing. I can tell their minds are totally absorbed in their conversation, and they are barely aware that I am in the room. I back out slowly.

"Thanks," Mom remembers to say as I leave.

Again, I listen at the door.

I hear Dad say, "I should have contacted you to see if you needed anything."

Now, that sounds encouraging.

I go back to the TV room.

"How goes it?" Aunt June says to me.

"Good, I think," I say, and smile.

Then we all become involved in watching George Burns and Gracie Allen, and for a while I forget everything else.

It must be around eight-thirty when the phone rings. I think briefly of Silver, but no, his dad probably won't let him call me long-distance. Aunt June answers the ring. In the TV room you can't normally hear a phone conversation from the October room, but suddenly I do hear Aunt June cry out, *"Oh, no!"*

Uncle Otis and Poppy exchange glances. Uncle Otis leaves the room. Aunt June stays on the phone for a few minutes longer. When she hangs up, I can hear Uncle Otis talking to her, but I can't hear his words. Then Poppy leaves the room too.

"Where's everybody going?" Avery wants to know.

Nobody answers him.

Now my curiosity gets the best of me. I go into the October room where I find Aunt June, Uncle Otis, and Poppy huddled together, whispering. When they see me, they stop abruptly.

"What's wrong?" I ask. "Who was on the phone?"

Aunt June's eyes are shiny with tears.

"Why are you crying?" I ask her.

She does not answer. I become aware of Emory and Avery at my elbow.

"Garnet, my sweet girl," Poppy says very softly, and something about his tone alarms me.

"What's wrong?" I ask.

"Will you and the boys go back in there and watch television for just a few more minutes?" Uncle Otis says gently. "Then we will . . ."

"Then you'll tell me what's wrong?" I ask.

They all nod yes.

"All right."

I nudge Emory and Avery back into the TV room where we sit down, but I can't concentrate on the show. I can't imagine what this is all about. In about ten minutes, Aunt June appears in the doorway.

"Garnet, honey, come with me," she says. "Emory, Avery, y'all stay here for now."

Aunt June places an arm around me and guides me through the October room, through the hallway and into the log room, where Poppy, Uncle Otis, Mom, and Dad are standing around silently. All eyes are on me.

"Sit here, sweetheart," Mom says, and motions me to the rocking chair.

I sit down. Mom stands on one side of me and places an arm across my shoulders. Dad stands on the other side. This is strange.

"What's going on?" I ask.

"Garnet, do you remember the minister at the Rugged Cross Chapel?" Aunt June asks me.

"Yeah, sorta. Why?"

"Well, his name is Mr. Greenleaf, and that was him on the phone. It seems he had some very bad news today." Aunt June pauses, takes a deep breath, then goes on. "And the youth minister—I forgot his name."

"Douglas," I say. "The youth minister is Douglas."

"Right," Aunt June says. "Douglas told Mr. Greenleaf that you should be notified about . . . this bad news."

"Me? How come?"

Aunt June looks at Mom, and Mom takes up the narrative. "Because it's about Silver and his dad, Garnet. There was an accident, and—"

"An accident? Is Silver hurt?"

At this point Mom takes one of my hands into hers.

"Will he be okay, Mom?"

"No, Garnet, he will not be okay. He . . ."

I see that Mom's eyes are brimming, and I begin to comprehend.

"Well, tell me!" I cry frantically. "What's happened?"

"As you know, Silver and his dad were driving very late last night," Mom says. "And it seems Mr. Shepherd fell asleep and went off the road."

"No!"

"Oh, Garnet, I'm so sorry! They didn't survive the crash."

27

I am in my bed. I have been in a strange kind of fitful sleep, stumbling through all the woods and roads and tunnels of my brain. There are places in here I have never seen before. Some of them are dark and creepy.

I see things from years ago. I had a good friend named Mary Ellen who just went away one day. Now here she is tucked away in one of these wrinkles in my brain.

Here is Mom crying in the moonlight.

And here is S.S.+A.R. circled by a heart.

I wake up. I am sweating. Mom is asleep beside me with one arm draped over me. It's too hot with her in my bed. I move her arm from me and throw off the sheet. I sit up. I see that an armchair has been pulled into my room, and Dad is sleeping in it.

"It's hot in here," I say.

Mom sits up on the side of the bed. There is a pan of water on my nightstand. She dips a cloth into it and bathes my face. She used to do this for me when I had a fever. Dad gets up and adjusts a fan on my dresser, so that the breeze falls more directly on me. Then he sits again in the armchair.

I lie back down. Why, oh why, oh why?

"Mom, why did this happen?"

"I don't know, Garnet. Sometimes life is a mystery."

She cools my face with the cloth.

"Silver calls me April," I say. "I want everybody to call me April. Okay, Mom?"

"Yes, of course," Mom says.

"You know something, Mom? His face lights up when he sees me," I go on. "When you were dating Dad, did his face light up for you?"

Mom pauses for a long time, and then she whispers, "Yes."

"Do you remember the first time Dad kissed you?"

Again she whispers, "Yes."

Dad shifts his weight in the chair.

I go back into the tunnels of my mind. There are question marks everywhere. Carved on all the trees. Scratched on the bridges. Painted on the road signs. Why? Why? Why? Some are healed. Some are taken. Why? Young people are not supposed to die. It makes no sense.

Later I wake to find Mom gone, but Dad is still in the chair. I can't tell if he's awake.

In the sweet by and by, we shall meet on that beautiful shore.

Is it true? Is there such a place where we will meet our loved ones again?

Now light is moving ever so slowly across the mountaintops. Mom and Dad are gone, and Poppy is in the chair.

"Hey, Poppy, you know what?"

"What, sweetheart?"

"I don't think we get any easy answers in this life. All we get is questions."

"I think you're right," he agrees, "but the important thing is that you keep on asking the questions."

Yes, I have to do my own search now—I must—and that's how I'll start, by questioning everything.

Later when I wake up, Poppy is sound asleep, and I have to go to the bathroom. I get up without waking him. I can hear a mourning dove somewhere outside. I touch the walls as I go down the hallway barefooted. The house seems to be alive and breathing. It's the pulse of my family, my people, all those who mean most to me in the world—here right now under this roof, just at the time I need them the most.

Is it true what Aunt June says, that everything happens for a reason?

I leave the bathroom, tiptoe down the stairs, and go

into the October room. There I find Mom and Dad curled up like spoons together on the forest green couch. Both are sound asleep. Last night I thought nothing would ever mean much to me again, but here is hope.

As I close the door quietly, the thought comes to me that I don't know the reason for Silver's death. I will probably never know. But I do know, without a doubt, there was a reason for his life.

Then I sit on the steps and cry, as a thin yellow beam of sunlight falls through the front window onto my face.

Go Fish!

GOFISH

RUTH WHITE

© William Anderson

What did you want to be when you grew up?
I wanted to be a movie star, of course. Didn't everybody?

When did you realize you wanted to be a writer?
I always wanted to be a writer, as well as a movie star. I made up stories and wrote them down as soon as I was able to write.

What's your most embarrassing childhood memory?
In second grade, I was busted for cheating on a spelling test. I was so ashamed, I never cheated again.

What's your favorite childhood memory?
On cold winter nights, curling up with my mother and sisters, all in one bed, while Mom read to us.

As a young person, who did you look up to most?
Teachers and preachers, because they were educated.

What was your favorite thing about school?
Recess and lunch. I was never a great student, but I did like reading.

What was your least favorite thing about school?
Arithmetic. I still don't get numbers.

What were your hobbies as a kid? What are your hobbies now?
I collected movie-star magazines and comic books. Today, I collect movies on DVD and audiobooks. So I haven't changed that much.

What was your first job, and what was your "worst" job?
My first job was babysitting. It paid fifty cents an hour. My worst job was working in the cafeteria in college.

How did you celebrate publishing your first book?
I went out to dinner with my family. I also bought myself a gold chain necklace that I still wear often.

Where do you write your books?
I used to write with a pen and paper while I sat in the middle of my bed. Today, I have an office with a computer in my home. It's easier, but it was more fun the other way.

What sparked your imagination for *A Month of Sundays*?
I wanted to write a book about small-town religious practices, and I also wanted to write a book about tragedy striking a very young person. The two themes fit well together.

Have you ever tried going to different churches like Aunt June?
Yes, I have been to many churches, but belonged to only two of them for brief periods of time. I find it stimulating to hear what

different churches say about the same subject. They are rarely the same. That's why it's important for a young person to ask a lot of questions as I suggest in my book, and make up his/her own mind.

Who was your first crush? What were they like?
I had crushes all through my school years. I don't even remember my first one. I do remember the first one that was reciprocated, and that was in high school. He was blond and cute and a football player. It was true love for three months. I think that's how first relationships are supposed to be. I thought I would never fall in love again until I did fall in love again and again. But I also remember a boy who was a neighbor and friend, but not a boyfriend, who was killed in a car crash at the age of eighteen. It was traumatizing.

Have you ever lived in a town like Black River, Virginia?
I lived in a town exactly like Black River, Virginia. I called it Coal Station in *Belle Prater's Boy*, Black Gap in *Weeping Willow*, Coaltown in *Sweet Creek Holler*, and Riverbend in *Tadpole*. Same town, different characters.

How do you feel about snakes?
I have always been afraid of snakes, even the non-poisonous ones. My own unreasonable prejudice.

Of the books you've written, which is your favorite?
Weeping Willow is my favorite because it is more true to life than any of my other books. It was a work of love.

What challenges do you face in the writing process, and how do you overcome them?
Distractions. Like other writers, I will find excuses not to get

down to work. Getting started is the most difficult part. Once you get into it, the story comes alive for you again, and the writing flows. I find if I can make myself write just one sentence, then just one more, I am on my way.

Which of your characters is most like you?
Tiny Lambert in *Weeping Willow*, also Ginny Shortt in *Sweet Creek Holler.*

What makes you laugh out loud?
When I was a kid, it was Abbott and Costello and the Three Stooges. Today, it's *America's Funniest Home Videos.*

What do you do on a rainy day?
About the same as any other day, except that I don't walk. I exercise indoors.

What's your idea of fun?
Going on a trip with my daughter and grandson. We recently went back to the mountains where I was born and raised. We saw my old high school and stayed in a cabin at the Breaks Interstate Park for three days, hiked, and had a picnic. That was fun.

What's your favorite song?
I have dearly loved so many songs over the years that it's hard to pick a favorite, but I would say my all-time favorite is "Bridge Over Troubled Water" from the '60s by Simon & Garfunkel. In the last few years, I have loved "After the Gold Rush" by Emmylou Harris, Linda Ronstadt, and Dolly Parton. The harmony is absolutely perfect.

Who is your favorite fictional character?
Probably Mick Kelly in *The Heart Is a Lonely Hunter.*

What was your favorite book when you were a kid? Do you have a favorite book now?

As a kid, the Laura Ingalls Wilder series, and now, *To Kill a Mockingbird*.

What's your favorite TV show or movie?

I like *American Idol* very much because I love to hear young, talented singers. Some favorite movies are *Blast from the Past*, *Yentl*, and *The Phantom of the Opera*.

If you were stranded on a desert island, who would you want for company?

Other than my daughter and grandson? Perhaps some really funny middle-school kids.

If you could travel anywhere in the world, where would you go and what would you do?

Italy, and I would travel around the countryside, staying at small village inns.

If you could travel in time, where would you go and what would you do?

I would go to the Middle Ages and try to teach people about cleanliness and health. Of course, I would probably be burned as a witch.

What's the best advice you have ever received about writing?

From Anne Lamott's book *Bird by Bird*, I learned not to be afraid of writing really bad first drafts. They are supposed to be bad. The good writing comes with editing those bad first drafts.

What do you want readers to remember about your books?
That, regarding place and time, most of them are authentic. These places and some of these characters actually lived.

What would you do if you ever stopped writing?
Die.

What do you like best about yourself?
My ability to change. It's a rare gift.

Do you have any strange or funny habits? Did you when you were a kid?
Yes and yes. I did and do make lists of everything, methodically planning my daily activities, my budget, my exercise routine, my diet.

What do you consider to be your greatest accomplishment?
Raising a beautiful, healthy, well-adjusted daughter who is a good citizen and an asset to society.

What do you wish you could do better?
Play the piano.

What would your readers be most surprised to learn about you?
That I totally dislike fantasy, vampires, and werewolves.

When Ruby sees the shadow of her dead pet goat Jethro dancing on his grave, it's clear that something strange is going on in Way Down Deep. As bad things start to happen, Ruby decides she must find answers.

Find the treasure and save the town in . . .

The Treasure of Way Down Deep

1

IT WAS SATURDAY, OCTOBER 2, 1954, IN WAY DOWN DEEP, West Virginia, and Ruby Jolene Hurley was celebrating her thirteenth birthday. It was a crisp autumn day, and the sky was a deep blue with a few puffy white clouds floating over the valley. Ruby was in her new room at The Roost, which was the boardinghouse where she had grown up. Only recently had she moved into this room, formerly occupied by Miss Worly, the town librarian. Miss Worly and Mr. Gentry, the high school band director, who had also lived at The Roost, had married and moved into a small house out on Highway 99.

"My spacious pastel boudoir" was how Miss Worly had described this room. She used that term, because, first of all, she liked peppering her sentences with fancy words, and, second, the room was decorated in pink and blue, with a dash of purple here and there, and it was larger than most of the other guest rooms at The Roost. Ruby loved the spacious pastel boudoir.

For a few minutes she lingered in front of the mirror before going downstairs to receive guests for her birthday party. Her new dress was the color of the golden maple leaves outside her window, and her shoes were black patent leather. Ruby's hair, of course, had always been a mass of red ringlets around her face, and her eyes were the color of bluebells. The people of Way Down considered her a natural beauty, but when she looked at her own image in the mirror, she was far more critical. She thought her hair was way too thick and wild, and too curly. And she thought she could have done without some of those freckles.

Downstairs in the common room Ruby found that her guests were arriving and were being greeted by Lucy Elkins and Ruby's Grandma Combs, both permanent residents of the boardinghouse. Miss Arbutus Ward, owner of The Roost, was also there. She was a direct descendant of Archibald Ward, who had first discovered Way Down Deep in the eighteenth century, and the last Ward still living in the town. Miss Arbutus had raised Ruby since she was a toddler and was like a mother to her.

The Reeders had come dressed in their finest, which wasn't to say much, but they were clean, and good-looking, every blessed one of them, starting with Peter, who was the same age as Ruby, and the boy she liked more than any other; Cedar, barely twelve; the identical twins Jeeter and Skeeter, nine; and the only girl, Rita, just turned six. They had moved to Way Down this past June when their stumpy little daddy, Robber Bob, had made a feeble attempt at robbing the bank—thus the nickname. Naturally, the bank president, Mr. Dales, had been so moved with pity for the desperate man that he had offered him the use of his own rental house, free of charge, until Robber

Bob could get back on his feet. Mayor Chambers, owner of the A&P, also gave him a job at the grocery store.

The eleven-year-old identical Fuller triplets came in next. They were Connie Lynn, Sunny Gaye, and Bonnie Clare, whose flaxen hair and blue eyes could light up a dark room. They were street evangelists who sang in three-part harmony as fine as the famous Andrews Sisters.

Next came Reese Mullins with some of his brothers and sisters. Reese used to fancy himself Ruby's beau, but that was before Peter Reeder came to town and stole her heart away.

After the Mullins children, Ruby was in such a whirlwind of greetings and giggles that she couldn't keep up with who had come in and who wasn't there yet. Of course every kid who lived in town *would* come. That's the way it was in Way Down. When you threw a party, you didn't have to send out invitations. You just told a few people, or you mentioned it over your telephone party line, and everybody got the message. You saved a lot of time that way.

Just then Rita approached Ruby and hugged her around the waist.

"Happy birthday, Ruby."

Rita was wearing a cute green and white pokey-dotted dress that Ruby had outgrown when she was six.

Ruby hugged her back.

Miss Arbutus and Ruby both had taken a shine to the little girl, and Rita had been spending every school night at The Roost in the tiny pansy-speckled room next door to Miss Arbutus, which used to be Ruby's room.

"So we can give her a good breakfast every morning," Miss Arbutus had explained to Rita's daddy, when asking his permission to keep the child, "and dress her pretty for school."

Robber Bob had agreed. He was tickled to see his only daughter get some feminine attention, since her own mother had died almost a year ago. Rita had started first grade in September, and Ruby and Miss Arbutus helped her with her schoolwork. They also introduced the little girl to their evening ritual of grooming and the sharing of confidences. When they were finished, and darkness had settled over their town nestled way down deep between the mountains, Ruby and Miss Arbutus would kiss Rita good night and hug each other. Then Ruby would go up to the second floor to visit with Grandma for a few minutes and give her a good-night hug as well before retiring to her spacious pastel boudoir, which was right beside Grandma's room.

Each Friday when school let out, six-year-old Rita would walk to her own house, just a hop and a skip up the street from The Roost, to spend the weekend with her daddy, Robber Bob; her addled granddaddy, Bird; and her four brothers. At dusk on Sunday evening Ruby would fetch her back to The Roost. It was an arrangement quite satisfactory to everybody concerned.

"I got you a present," Rita said to Ruby as she handed the older girl a small package wrapped in brown paper.

Not everybody was able to give Ruby a gift, but she didn't mind a bit. Inside the paper was an odd pewter-colored metal button with a hole in it.

Ruby was delighted. "What an uncommon thing!" And it really was. It looked like it might have come from a soldier's uniform.

"You can put a ribbon through the hole, and make a pretty necklace," Rita said proudly.

"What a good idea!" Ruby cried. "Thank you, Rita."

Carefully Ruby placed the metal button inside a small pocket in her new dress. Then she hugged the beaming little girl again.

"Let's play blind man's bluff!" somebody yelled.

Yes, they should start the games. What a grand party this was going to be!

After blind man's bluff, they played guess what?, then treasure hunt. It was during this game that the party expanded outdoors, because Miss Arbutus and Grandma had hidden some of the treasures in the yard.

Ruby and Peter were seated side by side in the common room, watching Skeeter and Jeeter tussle over a piece of bubble gum they had found in a vase, when suddenly Slim Morgan charged through the front door.

"Catastrophe!" he yelled. "Where's Ruby at?"

"I'm here, Slim. What'sa matter?"

"It's Jethro, Ruby. I think he's dead."

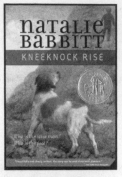